The Secret of the Circus

GORDON SNELL

POOLBEG

Published 1999 by
Poolbeg Press Ltd,
123 Baldoyle Industrial Estate,
Dublin 13, Ireland

© Gordon Snell 1999

The moral right of the author has been asserted.

The Arts Council
An Chomhairle Ealaíon

A catalogue record for this book is available from the British Library.

ISBN 1 85371 961 7

Cover illustration by Peter Hanan
Cover design by Artmark
Set by Rowland Phototypesetting Ltd in Stone Serif 9.5/14.5
Printed and bound by
Cox & Wyman Ltd., Reading, Berkshire.

www.poolbeg.com

About the Author

Gordon Snell is a well-known scriptwriter and author of books for children and adults. Other books in the series include *Dangerous treasure, The Mystery of Monk Island, The Curse of Werewolf Castle, The Phantom Horseman* and *The Case of the Mystery Graves*. He is also the author of *The Tex & Sheelagh Omnibus*. He lives in Dalkey, Co. Dublin, and is married to the writer Maeve Binchy.

For dearest Maeve, with all my love

CHAPTER ONE

Circus Plans

Brendan looked at his watch.

"The train's due in three minutes and forty-five seconds," he said.

His cousin Molly laughed. "Do you really think they keep such accurate timing?

Sometimes I think you're lucky if it gets here on the right day!"

It was the beginning of the summer holidays, and Brendan was down from Dublin to spend a few days with Molly and her family in Ballygandon. Their friend Dessy was due to join them, arriving on the afternoon train. Then their grandfather was coming to meet them in his car and take them for a drive before they all went back to tea at Molly's house.

"Now there are two minutes thirty-five seconds to go," said Brendan. "We should be able to hear it soon."

"Do you know if you put your hand on your ear and pull it forward, you can hear sounds at a bigger distance?" said Molly.

Brendan tried it. Then he tried pulling both ears forward. "I can't hear any better than usual," he said.

"Of course, you have to stand on one leg at the same time," said Molly.

Brendan nearly did so, but then he said: "You're codding me!"

Molly laughed. "Hey, I had you fooled there for a moment!"

"Not at all!" Brendan said loftily. "You're getting as bad as Dessy with all this joking around."

"No-one could rival Dessy," said Molly. "At this moment passengers are probably flinging themselves out of the train to avoid hearing any more of his jokes."

As the train came into the station, they could see the spiky hair of Dessy as he leaned out of the window, waving. He jumped off as soon as the train came to a stop, and nearly knocked into a large man in a tweed cap who was waiting to get on.

"Watch out!" the man snapped.

"Sorry,"said Dessy, and ran on to meet his friends. There were high-five greetings, and Dessy handed his blue hold-all to Brendan.

"There you are, my man," he said, "take that to my waiting Roller, would you?"

"In your dreams!" said Brendan, and threw the bag into the air. Dessy leaped up and caught it.

"Another spectacular save from the champ!" he cried, "and just as well too. There could have been precious pieces of glass in there."

"Precious pieces of chocolate, more likely," said Molly.

"No, I ate all that on the train," Dessy said, "but I'll show you what I do have." He put the bag down on the platform and unzipped it. He rummaged inside, and pulled something out. "Take a look at that!"

He held out a bright yellow yo-yo, with a clown's face painted on it. "This is state-of-the-art technology," he said. "Just watch!"

He put the loop of the string on his finger, and flicked the yo-yo so that it went down and rolled back up again. As it did so, it made a whizzing noise, and a light flashed inside the yellow cover.

"Brilliant," said Brendan.

"A-One," said Molly.

Dessy began to do tricks with the yo-yo, flinging it up into the air, curling it over his hand, and passing it behind his back.

"Let's have a go," said Brendan. But he had never mastered the skills of the yo-yo, and the wheel flopped down to the end of the string and stayed there. Molly's efforts weren't much better, and reluctantly they gave it back to Dessy who began doing tricks again.

"Grandpa Locky will be really impressed," said Molly. "Where is he, I wonder?"

"He should have been here by now," said Brendan. "He said he'd come and meet the train with us."

They waited in the yard outside the station. Dessy did his yo-yo tricks, telling jokes and riddles at the same time.

"Hey, I just made this one up on the way down here," he said. "What is a train driver's favourite kind of music?"

"OK, we give up," said Brendan.

Dessy grinned and said, "ROCK AND RAIL!" Brendan and Molly groaned. But they were saved from listening to any more of Dessy's jokes by the sight of an old blue car that came rattling up the road and stopped with a jerk in the yard. Out stepped their grandfather, Locky, his jaunty green hat on his head. He had on a tie that was even brighter than usual: it seemed to be in almost day-glo colours of red and yellow.

"Hi, Grandpa!" called Brendan and Molly.

"Well, well!" said Locky, "if it isn't that bunch of famous private eyes, the Ballygandon Gang! I'm sorry I'm late, but there's a very good reason, and I think you'll be excited to hear the news."

"What news?" asked Brendan.

"Have you had another win on the horses?" Molly wondered.

"I wish I had," said Locky. "But the last one I backed

4

is still running, I reckon – and the race started yesterday! No, this hasn't anything to do with horses – or not the racing kind, anyway. I was just coming through the town out on the Ballygandon road, when I saw a van parked, and a man sticking a poster to a telegraph pole."

"Was it for an election?" asked Dessy. "They plaster those all over Dublin. VOTE FOR DESSY, YOUR NUMBER ONE!"

"No, it was something much more exciting than politics," said Locky. "I got chatting to the man. Hans his name was, a nice fellow about my age – he said I could have one of the posters to show you. Come and have a look."

They followed him over to the car, and he reached in and took a big roll of paper out. He unrolled it and spread it on the bonnet of the car.

"A CIRCUS!" all three of them exclaimed together.

"That's right," said Locky, "and it's coming here." He pointed to a space at the bottom of the poster, where the name BALLYGANDON was written in big black letters, with dates underneath.

"That's next week!" said Molly eagerly.

"For two whole weeks!" cried Brendan.

They gazed at the poster with its colours even brighter than Locky's tie. It showed a large red-and-white striped tent, the Big Top as circus people called it. A banner flew over the top of the tent with the words "HANS

HOPPER'S CIRCUS" on it. On the bottom half of the poster there were pictures of a Ringmaster with top hat and whip, circus ponies prancing, a seal balancing a beach-ball on its nose, dogs jumping through hoops, a trapeze artist, and a clown juggling with clubs in the air.

"Are there any lions and tigers?" asked Brendan. "I always fancied myself as a lion-tamer."

"Nonsense," said Dessy, "you hide under the cinema seat when the MGM Lion roars!"

"I spy dinner!" Brendan gave a great roar and leaped at Dessy, his fingers stretched out like claws. He grabbed him and they wrestled, falling to the ground.

"Get up, you eejits," said Molly, pulling Brendan away. He and Dessy stood up, grinning.

Locky, who was used to this kind of behaviour, carried on calmly: "No, there aren't any lions and tigers, or elephants either. I talked to Hans Hopper the circus owner about that. He was the one putting up the posters. He said he'd never had wild animals like that in his circus, he thought it was cruel. So you'll have to find some other talent than lion-taming, Brendan."

"Well, I know what *I* can do, anyway," said Dessy.

"I don't think they have stand-up comics in the circus," said Locky.

"No, I mean *this*!" Dessy produced his yo-yo and began doing his tricks.

"That's very good," said Locky. "Maybe that juggling clown will take you on as his assistant."

"And with *his* face, Dessy wouldn't have to wear make-up!" said Brendan.

"Now how about that drive we were going on?" said Locky. "Let's take a trip around and see where we think the circus is going to be. It doesn't say on the poster."

The car bumped along the country roads around Ballygandon, while they tried to guess where the circus would be. The playing field seemed the most likely spot, but there were other places too. In fact it wasn't long before they found out.

Locky was driving along the road that ran at the foot of the hill where the ruined castle stood. The castle had been the scene of many adventures and dangers for the Ballygandon Gang. There had been some weird happenings too, unexplained sights and sounds – for the Castle was said to be haunted by the ghost of Princess Ethna, who was murdered there, centuries ago.

It looked peaceful enough now, its tumbledown tower pointing jaggedly into the blue sky. Locky stopped the car to let a woman in an anorak lead two big horses past them along the road. It was Mrs O'Rourke, who hired out horse-drawn caravans to holidaymakers. She had been involved in some shady goings-on in the past, especially when the Celtic brooch from the Ballygandon Hoard had been stolen.

Locky didn't like the woman, but he tried to be pleasant. He leaned out of the car window and said, "Good afternoon, Mrs O'Rourke, are you giving the horses a bit of exercise?"

"I'm moving them to another field," Mrs O'Rourke replied. "My field here is being hired out."

"By the Circus!" exclaimed Molly and Brendan together.

"That's right. They were lucky to get it. I have some big plans for that field, and there'll certainly be no room for a circus in future."

"Isn't that the field the local council want to make into a park and playground?" asked Locky.

Mrs O'Rourke was dismissive. "Oh, there was some talk of it, but there's no way they could afford the kind of money that field is worth."

Molly knew that her father and mother wouldn't be at all pleased by this news. They had been among the leaders of the campaign to get the field made into a park.

And indeed, as they sat down to tea, there was a great deal of anger at Mrs O'Rourke.

"That woman is a menace," said Molly's mother. "She doesn't care what she does just so long as she makes money."

"What plans do you think she has for the field?" Locky asked.

"Concreting it over to make a carpark, I shouldn't wonder," said Molly's father.

"Or a shopping centre?" said Molly.

"Oh, no, we don't need that!" said her mother.

"We'll have to stage a protest," said Molly.

"Well, nothing can happen till after the Circus has come and gone," said Locky. "In the mean time, maybe we can find out more about Mrs O'Rourke's plans."

"Yes, we'll get the Ballygandon Private Eyes on the trail," said Brendan.

After tea the three of them walked through the main street and out to the field below the castle. They stood there, imagining the huge tent which would soon be rising, the caravans and the big trucks, and the circus people preparing for their show.

"Look over there!" said Brendan suddenly. He pointed.

Standing leaning on a gate at the far end of the field was Mrs O'Rourke, and beside her was a man they knew only too well – one of the most unscrupulous and crafty characters in the whole area: Seamus Gallagher.

"Well, whatever her plans are," said Molly, "you can bet that if Seamus is mixed up in them, they're probably against the law!"

CHAPTER TWO

Roll Up! Roll Up!

The next morning, in the yard outside Molly's parents' shop, the Ballygandon Gang were making plans to become circus performers.

"It shouldn't be a problem," said Dessy confidently. "After all, we got parts in the movie when that was made here."

"And we were very good, too," said Molly. "I played the tin whistle in that, maybe I could do the same in the circus." She got out her tin whistle and began to play a fast tune. Brendan and Dessy linked arms and started to do what they thought was a clattering *Riverdance*-style step.

After a while they stopped, out of breath.

"You lads will have to get into training," said Molly.

"I think I'll do my yo-yo act instead," Dessy decided.

"And perhaps I could do some bareback riding on the ponies," said Molly, who was quite an expert on horseback. "Remember the time I rode Rory, pretending to be the Phantom Horseman?"

"That's settled, then," said Dessy. "What are you going to do, Brendan?"

Brendan couldn't think of anything he was good at, except football. He picked up the ball that was lying in a corner of the yard. "I could do some fancy footwork with this," he said.

"That's it!" said Molly, "you can do tricks with the ball – but not with your feet."

"What do you mean?"

"Use your nose!" said Molly. "Like the seal on the poster, balancing the beach ball."

"Don't be ridiculous," said Brendan.

"Go on, give it a try," said Dessy. "Bet you can't balance it on your nose for ten seconds."

Brendan would never turn down a challenge. He picked the ball up, put his head back, and placed the ball on his nose. It was mucky and smelly, but he persevered.

Taking his hands away, he began to stagger backwards and forwards, trying to keep the ball in place.

Dessy and Molly counted: "One! Two! Three! . . ."

The ball rolled a bit and Brendan had to tilt his head and hold the ball on his closed right eye. "Ten!" shouted the other two, just as the ball rolled off and he fell to his knees.

He looked up to see his mother gazing down at him with astonishment.

"Well, Brendan," she said, "that's the first time I've seen anyone trying to dribble the ball with their head!"

Brendan had forgotten that his mother was coming down to take Locky up to Dublin for his annual medical check-up. She had called at Ballygandon to see her sister, on the way to collect Locky at Horseshoe House, the residential home he lived in. She had been planning to bring Brendan and Dessy back to Dublin too.

Now he would have to do some heavy persuading, so that they could stay in Ballygandon for the Circus. There was no way they were going to miss that.

His mother said, "I'm just going to have a chat and a cup of tea with Maureen, and then we'll be on our way. So you lads had better pack your things."

"Well Mam," said Brendan, "you see, there's been a bit of a change of plan . . ."

He explained about the Circus, and how they were even hoping they might be able to perform in it.

"We'll be a smash hit," said Dessy, "I'll do my yo-yo tricks, Molly has her tin whistle, and Brendan has his . . ." He paused.

"His Nose Balancing Act!" said Molly.

Brendan's mother smiled. She remembered how much she had loved the Circus as a child. "All right," she said, "as long as you're no trouble to Maureen."

"Oh, they won't be," said Molly, "they're little angels, believe me!"

"There's no need to overdo it, Molly," said Mrs O'Hara, going indoors.

"That's wonderful!" said Brendan. "We can stay for the Circus!"

"We'd better get practising," said Dessy.

Brendan picked up the football and looked at it doubtfully. "I'm not sure ball-balancing is really so entertaining," he said. "I know! I'll be a tightrope-walker instead."

"I'll get some rope from the shop," said Molly. "We can string it way up there over the yard, between the big tree and the roof of the house."

"Let's wait a bit," said Brendan hastily. He already felt a bit dizzy at the thought.

"I'll start practising by walking along the fence."

He went down to the open gate which led on to the road, and climbed on to the wooden railing of the fence beside it. He stood up, wobbling a little. Then he put his arms out at the side to steady himself, and began slowly to put one foot in front of the other.

"Hey, that's good, Brendan!" said Dessy.

"I heard of a man once who tightrope-walked across Niagara Falls," said Molly. "Maybe we can string a rope across the river for *you!*"

The thought made Brendan feel dizzy again, but he kept going. Then he stopped suddenly, gazing down the road. "Wow!" he exclaimed. "Get a look at that!"

"What?" asked Molly. She and Dessy went towards

him, as Brendan jumped down from the fence, and pointed.

"That car coming towards us," said Brendan. "Isn't that a beauty?"

The three of them leaned over the fence, peering down the road. Approaching them was a gleaming dark green car with a silver emblem on the front.

"That's a Jaguar," said Brendan. "You'd need to win the Lotto to afford one of them."

"That reminds me," said Dessy. "What did the man say when they asked him how he liked his new jaguar?"

"You're going to tell us, aren't you, Dessy?" said Molly.

"He said, 'I don't like it much, it growls a lot. I'm thinking of getting a car instead'."

Molly and Brendan laughed. "You should tell that to the fella who's driving this one," said Brendan. "Look, he seems to be slowing down."

"What would a fancy car like that be doing in Ballygandon?" Molly wondered.

"I don't know," said Brendan, "but it's pulling up right here."

The Jaguar came to a stop outside the gate. A tall man with black wavy hair and a moustache stepped out and came towards them. He was wearing a smart blue blazer, and he had a roll of paper under his arm.

"Hello, kids," he said. "Is this your place?"

"That's right," said Molly, "it's my family's shop, and that's our house behind it."

"Be a good girl," said the man, "and run and ask your parents if I can put a poster on their fence, announcing the Circus."

"You're from the Circus?" asked Brendan. He wondered what kind of performer this smooth-looking character could be.

"Right in one, sonny," said the man.

Molly didn't like adults who called people "sonny" and "good girl" – but she said nothing. She went across the yard and into the shop, half hoping her parents would say no.

"Nice car, mister," said Dessy. "Must have cost a packet."

"It did," said the man.

Dessy took the yo-yo from his pocket and began doing tricks. The man glanced at him, then looked at his watch.

"Hey, mister," said Dessy desperately, "what do you get if you put an elephant in the fridge?"

"I don't know and I don't want to know," said the man. "What's keeping that girl?"

Just then Molly came out of the shop and across the yard. "They say it's OK to put it on the fence beside the gate," she said.

"Right," said the man. He unrolled the poster and said, "Hold this."

Brendan didn't like being ordered about, but he took hold of the poster and he and Molly unrolled it. The man took some big drawing pins out of his pocket, and said, "OK, hold it up against the fence."

As he pinned the poster up, Dessy, still smarting from his brush-off, asked: "Well, what do *you* do in the Circus then, mister?"

"I am Enzio the Ringmaster," the man said. "I run the whole show."

"But our grandfather met Mr Hopper," said Molly. "It's his Circus, isn't it?"

"That's only the name," said Enzio. "I'm in charge of it all."

"Do you need any extra people?" Molly asked. "Like bareback riders, tin whistle players, yo-yo artists . . . ?"

"We don't employ children," said the man, going towards his car. "Come back when you grow up."

As Enzio was getting into the car, Brendan called out: "Any chance of some free tickets, mister?"

"No way," said Enzio. "We've got to make a living." The Jaguar purred away down the road.

"What a charmer!" said Molly sourly.

"What was all that about him being in charge?" asked Brendan, "and Hans Hopper being only the name? Grandpa met him, and from what he told us, Mr Hopper seemed to be the owner of the whole thing."

"It all sounds a bit fishy," said Molly. "We'll ask Grandpa Locky more when he comes back tomorrow."

"By the way, Dessy," said Brendan, "what *do* you get if you put an elephant in the fridge?"

"Footprints in the butter," said Dessy.

The next afternoon, when Brendan's mother brought Locky to call on the way back to Horseshoe House, Brendan, Molly and Dessy crowded round the car as it stopped in the yard.

"Are you OK, Grandpa?" Molly asked.

"Fit as a fiddle!" said Locky. "The doctor was delighted with me."

"There's something we wanted to ask you," said Brendan.

"Later, Brendan," said Brendan's mother. "Give him a chance to get his breath. Come on inside and have a rest, Dad."

"I'm not out of breath," said Locky, "and I don't need a rest. I'll join you inside in a couple of minutes."

Brendan's mother sighed, and went indoors.

Brendan said, "We wanted to ask you more about Mr Hopper and the Circus. You see, we met . . ."

Locky interrupted him. "I can tell you a lot more about Mr Hopper. I met him by chance in the hospital in Dublin. He'd been taken in the day before – an emergency.

He suddenly had bad stomach pains. He's recovering now, but they're keeping him in for a few days to check him out for ulcers and such like."

"What about the Circus?" asked Molly.

"His assistant Enzio will look after it for the moment," said Locky.

"It sounded as though Enzio thought he was looking after it for good," said Brendan.

"What do you mean?"

They told Locky all about their meeting with Enzio.

Locky said, "And he definitely said Hans Hopper was only the name, and he was running it?"

"Definitely," said Brendan. "He never said anything about Mr Hopper being sick."

"Very odd," said Locky. "I'm sure Hans won't be too pleased if he hears Enzio is throwing his weight about like that. Maybe we can investigate more when the Circus comes to town."

"The Ballygandon Gang will be on the case," said Molly.

"And we won't have to wait very long," said Dessy excitedly. "Listen to that!"

A blast of brassy circus music could be heard in the distance. They ran down to the gate and looked down the road. Two horses were prancing with a small open carriage behind them. And behind that they could see, stretching away down the road, a long procession of caravans and huge trucks.

Standing in the front carriage, holding the reins, was a tall woman with long blonde hair and a silver top hat on her head. She was dressed in a skin-tight outfit covered in red, yellow and blue sequins that flashed in the sunlight. She was holding a microphone, and above the music her voice could be heard loud and clear from the loudspeakers: "ROLL UP! ROLL UP! ROLL UP! THE CIRCUS IS COMING TO TOWN! ROLL UP, ROLL UP, AND SEE THE GREATEST SHOW ON EARTH!"

CHAPTER THREE

Plots Overheard

"Come on, let's join the procession!" cried Molly, and they ran out of the gate.

They jogged along beside the trotting horses at the front, and Molly imagined herself sitting, or even standing, on the back of one of them, as it pranced around the circus ring. She'd be dressed in a glittering costume like the top-hatted woman, and the crowd would roar and cheer.

"Giddy-up! Giddy-up!" she called.

The tall woman looked down at her and snapped: "Don't frighten the horses!"

Molly stopped, and scowled. The horses weren't frightened at all. She was about to shout something rude back at the woman, but she didn't want to make an enemy of her right at the start. After all, she wanted to make friends with those horses, and then she might even be allowed to ride them.

21

Brendan and Dessy had stopped too. The three of them watched the caravans and trucks go by. They all had HANS HOPPER'S CIRCUS in big bright letters on the side. Circus people leaned out of the cars and caravans and threw sweets to them. On the side of one big truck were the words, MADAME GAZEBA'S PERFORMING DOGS AND SEALS. In the passenger seat of the car drawing the caravan sat a woman with a bright orange feather scarf round her neck. She had a long pointed nose and bright red lipstick, and her black hair was done up in an elaborate pile on top of her head.

"That must be Madame Gazeba herself," said Dessy. "She looks really hoity-toity."

As she passed them, Madame Gazeba looked out and gave a royal wave of her hand.

"Game ball, Duchess!" cried Dessy, and made a sweeping bow. Madame Gazeba gave him a lofty smile.

"She's got performing dogs," said Molly thoughtfully. "Maybe we could train Tina to do some tricks for the circus."

"The only trick Tina does is to sleep all day," said Brendan.

"She's a very intelligent dog," said Molly.

"She just hides it well," said Dessy. Then seeing Molly's temper beginning to rise, he added hastily: "Only joking! Tina's as bright as a hundred-watt bulb!"

Molly grunted. Then Brendan said excitedly, "Hey, look at that!"

An open truck was approaching. The back of it was packed with crates and bundles, and sitting cross-legged on the top bundle was a clown. He had a big red coat with white and green spots on it, a large floppy yellow bow tie, and a battered bowler hat with a tall white feather sticking up from it.

He was juggling with four green clubs which he was tossing in the air in turn and catching. The three of them clapped and shouted encouragement. The clown caught all four clubs and held them in one hand. With the other he lifted his hat. His head was covered with a bright orange wig full of curls. He held out his hat and smiled, the exaggerated made-up red lips making his mouth seem huge.

"Thank you, ladies and gentlemen!" he called. Then he threw the hat in the air, where it turned over a couple of times, then landed back on his head. They clapped even louder.

As the end of the procession approached, Brendan said, "Let's cut across to the field while they go through the town, then we'll be ready to meet them."

They were just about to set off when they saw, at the end of the procession, the sleek green Jaguar with Enzio at the wheel.

"Well, I'm not going to cheer *him*, that's for sure," said Dessy. Enzio didn't even glance in their direction. He suddenly hooted the horn of the Jaguar, and revved it up. He pulled out into the road on the right of the last truck, and roared off ahead, overtaking the procession.

"Show-off!" said Molly.

"And look who's coming to join the procession now," said Brendan. They looked down the road. A Land-Rover was coming towards them. A bald man with an angry red face was driving it, and in the back seat was a large Alsatian dog.

"It's Seamus Gallagher," said Molly. "What's he tagging along for?"

As the Land-Rover was beside them, Brendan called: "Hi, Seamus! Have you come to join the Circus?"

"The other clown's further ahead!" said Dessy.

Seamus turned and scowled at them as he drove on.

"Well, I hope he's not planning to put that horrible dog Lonnigan into the show," said Molly. "He'd have the tent chewed up before you'd know it!"

They made their way through the back lanes and across the fields, till they came to a hedge beside the road that led to the big field where the circus would be. They were about to scramble through a gap in the hedge when they saw a van approaching. It stopped not far from the gate into the field. Mrs O'Rourke stepped out. She went over to the gate and undid the chain. Then with some effort she pushed the heavy gate wide open, ready for the circus vans to enter.

They decided to wait behind the hedge, until the procession arrived. If they appeared Mrs O'Rourke would no doubt tell them to clear off. She didn't like the Bally-gandon Gang one bit.

Mrs O'Rourke glanced over towards the town, where the blaring music and the cries of "ROLL UP! ROLL UP!" could be heard in the distance. Then she leaned into the van and produced a big map which she spread out on the bonnet. It looked like the map they had seen her examining with Seamus.

Mrs O'Rourke had one finger on the map. She kept looking across the field, then tracing a line with her finger across the map.

"I wonder what she's up to," said Molly.

"And what *he's* up to, as well," said Brendan, looking down the road. They saw the green Jaguar driven by Enzio coming along the road. He had come on ahead of the circus cavalcade. Mrs O'Rourke saw it too. To their surprise, she quickly rolled up the map and stowed it back in the van.

The Jaguar came to a smooth halt behind Mrs O'Rourke's van.

Enzio got out and came towards her. They shook hands.

"The field's all ready for you," said Mrs O'Rourke.

"Thank you," said Enzio. "We're on our way. Now if we could just go and check the markers we made the other day for where the Big Top will go . . ."

"Certainly," said Mrs O'Rourke. Enzio began to go through the gate, but Mrs O'Rourke stopped him.

25

"Before we start . . ."

"Yes?"

"Well, you recall the financial arrangements we agreed?"

"Of course."

"I think in business dealings of this kind, it's customary to provide a certain amount of cash 'up-front', as they say."

"Is that what they say?" sneered Enzio. "You'll get your money, don't worry. Even if it is more than the field is worth."

"I'm sure I will," said Mrs O'Rourke, "but I think it would be only fair to have, say, a quarter of it first? As a seal on the bargain."

"And what if I say no?"

"It could make it a little difficult. After all, your whole mob is just coming down the road now. I doubt if you'll find another place at such short notice."

"Outrageous!" said Enzio. But he groped in his pocket and produced a large bundle of notes. He peeled off several of them and thrust them towards Mrs O'Rourke. She took them and smiled.

"Thank you," she said, putting them into the pocket of her anorak. "Now, let's go, shall we?" They went through the gate.

"She's money-mad, that woman," said Molly.

"I'd say there's a pair of them in it there," said

26

Brendan, as they stepped through a gap in the hedge on to the road, ready to greet the Circus.

The scene as the Circus moved in was like a show in itself. There were arguments about which caravans should go where, trucks got bogged down in mud, the tent-men shouted at people to get out of the way as they lugged the poles and ropes and huge panels of striped canvas into place, ready to put up the Big Top.

The Ballygandon Gang wandered around, unnoticed, watching it all excitedly.

They peered through a gap in the side of one truck and were surprised to see a shallow pool with two seals flopped in it, apparently asleep.

From another truck they heard the yapping of dogs.

"That must be Madame Gazeba's Performing Dogs," said Molly. And indeed, from a caravan beside the truck they saw Madame Gazeba emerge, carrying a plastic lunch-box. She climbed up some steps that led to a door in the side of the truck and went inside. They went across and listened.

"There, there, Tizzy Wizzy," they heard her say, "Didn't you like the journey? And what about you, Toozy Woozums? Never mind, Mammy's here to give you a yummy yummy treat." The dogs had stopped yapping, and were now making little squeals of delight.

"So the Duchess has a heart of gold after all," Molly smiled.

They went on strolling around among the trucks and caravans, watching the bustle of unloading and erecting, as the circus people rushed about. It looked chaotic, but they could see that everyone knew their job and they were getting on with it, even if they shouted and swore while they did it.

Then, coming round the corner of a caravan, Molly who was in front motioned to them to stop. They held back, peering around the corner. Near the entrance to the caravan stood two people. One was Enzio and the other was the woman in the spangled outfit who had led the procession. She was trying to clutch Enzio and draw him towards her.

"Not now, Paula!" said Enzio. "There'll be time for that later."

"You're trying to give me the brush-off!" said Paula. "I know what it is, it's that O'Rourke woman who hired you the field. You fancy her, don't you?"

"I do in my hat!" snarled Enzio. "I did a deal with her, that's all."

"And what did this 'deal' involve? You're a fool, Enzio. Our whole plan could be banjaxed if you go fooling around like that."

"You're just jealous," said Enzio. "The plan is fine. Hans is away out of the picture, and with any luck that's where he'll stay. It's our show, now."

"You mean that?" asked Paula.

"Of course I do."

"And I'll be the star?"

"Yes, yes, yes! Just as soon as I get rid of Andy."

"The sooner the better."

"I couldn't agree more. But we need to be careful. Believe me, my love, it won't be long before your name is up there in lights as the star of the show."

"And yours as the owner of the whole shoot!"

"We're on our way," said Enzio, embracing her.

"See you later, Ringmaster!" Paula gave him a wink, and went into the caravan.

They watched Enzio stride off to organize the setting up of the Big Top.

"The plot thickens," said Dessy.

"Those two are a pair of villains, I'd say," said Brendan.

They moved along the line of caravans. Suddenly they heard a voice say, "Hi there!"

From the window of one of the caravans came the head of the clown they had seen in the procession. He had taken off his wig, and was wiping at his make-up with a cloth. He was a lot younger than they had thought.

"I saw you cheering me on beside the road, didn't I?" he said.

"That's right," said Molly. She told him their names, and he reached out his hand and shook theirs.

"I'm very pleased to meet you," he said. "Won't you come in for a chat?"

"We'd love to," said Brendan.

"Great," said the clown. "Oh, by the way – my name is Andy."

CHAPTER FOUR

Meeting the Clown

They went up the steps into Andy's caravan. They were in a living-room area which took up half of the total space inside. It was a bit like stepping into a magical cave. There were multi-coloured helium balloons on the ceiling, the blue walls were painted with golden stars, and there was a toy parrot in a cage. Clown hats and curly wigs hung on hooks on one wall, and against the wall opposite, there was a metal rail on a stand, and hanging on it was a row of bright clown costumes.

On the floor below were some of the oddest shoes they had ever seen. They were special clown shoes: one pair was over half a metre long, with flaps on the toes, another looked like leather boots for a giant, and another had tall stilts sticking up out of the shoes.

Andy saw them gazing around in wonder. "This is my dressing-room for the show," he said, "as well as my travelling house. Make yourselves at home. There are some minerals in the fridge there."

"Thanks, Andy." They sat at a table and sipped lemonade, while Andy sat down at a dressing-table with a mirror that had lights all around the frame. He dipped a cloth into a large open jar of face-cream and began to wipe the rest of the make-up off his face.

"Do you put on a different clown face each time?" Brendan asked.

"No, always the same one. It's a rule of the profession. Each clown designs his own make-up, and then it's kept in a register and no-one else can use exactly that one."

They watched him as he transformed himself back into an ordinary person. His face was open and friendly, and his eyes were a twinkly blue. His smile was nearly as broad as his clown smile had been.

He got up from the dressing-table and went across to the fridge. "I think I'll have a drink myself," he said.

They looked at one another. "Do you think we should tell him what we heard?" Brendan whispered.

"I think we've got to," said Molly.

"What are you lot whispering about?" Andy asked, as he sat down at the table with a can of beer.

"It's something we overheard just now, outside there," said Molly.

"Something about *you*," said Brendan.

They told Andy about the conversation between Enzio and Paula. He frowned.

"I know that pair don't like me," said Andy. "Paula wants to do a juggling act, as well as ride round on the ponies, so she can claim to be the real star, and leave me with just a bit of slapstick clowning."

"It sounded more as if they want to get you out of the show altogether," said Brendan.

"Maybe," said Andy. "but Paula's really not much of a juggler, unless you like the sound of twirling plates crashing to the ground. Hans knows that, and he'd never put her in my place. Hans is a great guy. He really looks after all his people."

"But Hans is sick, and away in Dublin," said Molly, "and I think Enzio and Paula may have plans to take over the circus completely."

"Hey," said Dessy, "do you think he was *made* sick, on purpose?"

"What do you mean?" Andy asked.

"Well, maybe that stomach upset was not an accident. Perhaps someone put poison in his food."

"Surely they wouldn't go as far as that?" Andy was horrified.

"They sounded pretty ruthless to me," said Dessy.

"I think we should warn Hans," said Molly.

"We'll go up to Dublin and see him in the hospital," said Brendan.

"He doesn't know us," said Molly, "why should he

33

believe a bunch of kids, even if we were let in to see him at all?"

"They'd let Locky in," said Brendan. "He's met him. Let's ask him to take us up to Dublin tomorrow."

"Your mother's only just brought him back," Molly said.

"He won't mind," said Dessy, "Locky loves a bit of excitement."

"Hey, I've just thought of something," said Brendan, "Locky's with my mother at your house right now, Molly. She's taking him to Horseshoe House and then back to Dublin. Maybe she'd bring me home with her, and bring Locky back too."

"Great idea," said Dessy.

"We can go to the hospital and see Hans tomorrow, then come back here on the train," said Brendan.

"Molly and I will stay and investigate," said Dessy. "We may be able to pick up some clues."

"You sound like a bunch of real detectives," Andy smiled.

"We are," said Molly, "we're the Ballygandon Gang Private Eyes."

"Let us tell you about some of the cases we've cracked," said Dessy eagerly.

"There was this movie about werewolves being made here . . ."

"I'd better be going," said Brendan, though he was reluctant to miss out on the stories. "I want to catch

34

Mam and Locky before they leave." He went to the door.

As he reached it, the door opened and a face peered in. It was a man with a mop of wild red hair, a droopy ginger moustache and staring green eyes. Brendan stepped back in astonishment.

"Hi there, Dragon-Man," said Andy. "Come in and meet my new friends, the Ballygandon Gang."

The Dragon-Man came in. He was a big, burly man dressed like a wrestler, with black tights and boots, and a red vest with a picture on the chest of a fierce green dragon breathing fire.

The Dragon-Man's greeting was like a long-drawn-out roar: "HAAAAAAA-LO THERE!"

They introduced themselves.

"The Dragon-Man does a fire-eating act," Andy explained.

Brendan was even more reluctant to leave now, but he was committed to the plan, so he said goodbye and went out.

When he got back to Molly's house, his mother and Locky were just about to leave.

"Well, thanks for coming back to say goodbye," said Brendan's mother, somewhat sarcastically. "We hardly see you at home at all, these holidays."

"If it's all right, Mam," said Brendan. "I thought I'd come home with you now."

"Of course it's all right." His mother was pleased. But

she was less pleased when he explained that he'd like Locky to come back too.

"I've just brought him down here!" she exclaimed.

"I know, but you see . . ." Brendan explained it was urgent they go to see Hans and warn him about what was happening in the Circus. Locky was at once enthusiastic, but Brendan's mother took some persuading. Finally she agreed.

She looked at Locky and Brendan and said: "You're as bad as each other, you two."

"Yes, there's a pair of them in it, all right," said Molly's mother.

"OK, get in the car," said Brendan's mother.

Back at the caravan, Molly and Dessy told of the earlier adventures of the Ballygandon Gang.

"Well, you've certainly cracked a few problems in your time," said Andy admiringly.

"I'm sure we'll crack this problem too," said Molly.

"What problem's that?" asked the Dragon-Man.

Andy said hastily: "Oh, it's nothing to worry about, just . . . some petty thieving that's been going on round here."

Molly and Dessy realised he didn't want to say too much about their suspicions to the Dragon-Man. They wondered if Andy thought he might be mixed up in the plot.

Molly decided to change the subject. She asked: "What exactly do you do in your circus act?"

"I'll show you," said the Dragon-Man. "Step outside."

He led them along the row of caravans, and stopped at one which had the same dragon emblem as his vest, painted on the side.

"Wait here," he said, going inside.

"You'll enjoy this," said Andy. "The Dragon-Man is the best in the business."

When he stepped out of the caravan, the Dragon-Man was carrying a small metal can. "Time to light the fire!" he cried.

He struck a pose with his legs apart and his head back. He unscrewed the cap of the can and took a swig from it. Then he took from his pocket a big box of matches.

"Hold this," he told Dessy. Dessy held the box, and the Dragon-Man took out a long match. He chanted:

"Fire and flame is my game!

Dragon-Man is my name!"

Then he struck the match, and as Dessy and Molly gasped, he stuck the flame into his mouth. Immediately he took it away, and breathed out a great jet of fire into the air. He struck another match and did the same thing.

Dessy and Molly clapped loudly. The Dragon-Man took a bow.

"That was wonderful," said Molly.

"Isn't your mouth burnt to a crisp?" asked Dessy.

"Not at all," said the Dragon-Man. "I've got a tongue of steel."

"What's the trick of it?" asked Molly.

"Oh, I can't tell you that," said the Dragon-Man. "Trade secrets, you know. But it's a great advantage when you're eating curry! Which reminds me, I must go and get something to eat."

"What do you eat, besides fire?" asked Dessy with interest.

"Hamburgers mainly. They're easy to cook. I just breathe on them!" He let out a dragon-style roar, laughed, and walked off.

"So you're from Ballygandon yourselves?" asked Andy.

"I am," said Molly. "Dessy and Brendan come from Dublin, but we let them hang around here. We're very easy-going in the country."

Dessy made a face. Andy said: "Maybe you'd like to show me round?"

"Sure," said Molly. "We'll give you the guided tour."

"Fine," said Andy. "Let's start with the castle up there."

They climbed the winding path up the hill and went through the gap in the wall that led into the ruins. Even though it was a fine day, the air inside the castle walls felt strangely cool and clammy. They wandered across the straggly grass and the bare patches of earth, scattered with fallen stones. One wall had a big arched window, gaping to the sky. There was a huge open fireplace big enough to stand inside and look up the dark chimney to the clouds sailing high above.

Then they came to the ruined tower which poked up high into the air like a broken steeple. There was an entrance at the bottom and inside, a stone staircase led upwards. Andy was about to go up it, when Molly said: "It's dangerous up there. The stones are slippery, and the stairs just end in empty air."

"That's where the ghost of Princess Ethna walks at midnight," said Dessy dramatically.

"Who was she?" asked Andy.

They told him the legend about the Princess who had come to marry the son of the O'Brien chief who was the lord of the castle. At the feast on the night before the wedding she had been found murdered on the stairs of the tower, stabbed with her own Celtic brooch. There had been a bloody feud between her clan and the O'Briens that had lasted for years.

"It's strange," said Molly, "but I've just remembered another story that's connected with Ethna. There was a jester in the castle who juggled with clubs just like you. And his name was Andreas."

"Andy for short," said Andy.

"That's weird all right," Dessy said.

"The story goes," said Molly, "that he was juggling below the tower, trying to warn Princess Ethna who was at the top. Suddenly as he threw up his silver-handled clubs, they seemed to disappear into thin air. Then, while he was searching for them, there was a scream from the tower, and he knew it was too late to save Ethna. She had been killed."

"What happened to Andreas?"

"He ran for his life," said Molly.

"And what about the clubs?"

"They were never found. But they found Andreas, and thought he was part of the plot. So they killed him."

CHAPTER FIVE

Ponies and Dogs

"Surprise, surprise!" said Brendan's mother to his father when they got back home to Dublin.

"Locky, you're back – did you miss us already?" Brendan's father laughed. "And Brendan, you're home too. This *is* an honour!"

"Hi, Dad!" said Brendan.

"Well, I need a cup of tea after all that traipsing around the countryside," said Brendan's mother. She went off to the kitchen.

Locky and Brendan explained to Brendan's father that they were going to visit Hans the circus-owner in hospital the next day, and they told him too about their suspicions of Enzio.

"Whereabouts in Ballygandon is the Circus setting up?" asked Brendan's father.

"In the field just below the old castle," said Locky.

"They're paying Mrs O'Rourke a lot of money to hire

it," said Brendan. "Everyone in Ballygandon wants that field to be made into a park and a playground, but we think Mrs O'Rourke has some other plan for it. Seamus Gallagher seems to be mixed up in it, too."

"That crook?" Brendan's father said. "I seem to remember he's been mixed up in a lot of scams and skulduggery in that part of the world. Listen, through my newspaper work I've got a few contacts in the planning office. I'll see what I can find out. It may take a while, though."

"I'm not sure how long we've got," said Brendan.

"Well, she can't do anything till after the Circus has left town," said Locky. "They're there for two weeks."

"I'll see what I can do."

At the hospital next morning, Hans was delighted to see Locky again. He said he felt better, and should be out in a few days. They still weren't certain what had caused the stomach pains, and they wanted to do some more tests.

Locky said, "I'd like you to meet my grandson Brendan, a founder member of the famous Ballygandon Gang."

"That sounds very terrifying," said Hans, shaking hands with Brendan.

"Oh, they're not thugs," said Locky, smiling. "They're a bunch of Private Eyes.

42

And seriously, we want to tell you some of the things they've been finding out."

Hans listened, frowning. Then he shook his head and said: "I think you must be mistaken. I can't believe that Enzio and Paula would be plotting against me. Of course I know they fancy each other, but there's nothing wrong with that."

"But what about Andy?" said Brendan. "She wants to take over his juggling act."

"That can't be so," said Hans. "Andy's one of the best jugglers there is. I brought him into my team when he was just a youngster. I could see what a talent he had. He's a natural, no one could ever replace him."

"Paula thinks she will."

"You've no proof of all this," said Hans.

"We're doing our best to find some," said Brendan.

"Well, until you do . . ." Just then the mobile phone on Hans's bedside table gave a shrill ring.

The man in the next bed looked up from his newspaper and glowered across at Hans. "Noisy damned gadgets!" he muttered. "They ought to be banned."

"Sorry," said Hans politely. "Only my Circus people have this number." Then he said into the phone, "Oh, hello, Enzio. Thanks, I'm getting on fine . . . A few days, they say . . . No, they don't know what it was, exactly . . . It's kind of you to worry . . . And thanks for sending in the box of chocolates . . ."

Locky and Brendan exchanged glances. They knew

just how insincere Enzio's concern was. Brendan looked at the chocolate box beside the bed, wondering if it was part of Enzio's plot. Hans went on talking to Enzio about the preparations for the opening performance. Finally he said: "I'm delighted everything's going so well, Enzio, and thanks for holding the fort for me. I'll be thinking of you all tomorrow. Good luck!" He switched off the phone. The man in the next bed rattled his newspaper but said nothing.

"No problems there," said Hans. He saw Brendan and Locky looking downcast.

"It's good of you to worry," he went on, "and just to reassure you, I'll give you my mobile phone number so that if you do find out anything, you can let me know.

But I'm sure there's nothing to find, believe me."

He wrote down the number, then said: "Why don't you have these? It was a kind thought of Enzio's, but I don't really like chocolates." He gave them the box and they said goodbye.

Molly and Dessy called on Andy in his caravan. He was just going out to do a bit of practising. They watched him twirling the clubs with uncanny skill.

"I'm afraid that beats even my yo-yo tricks," said Dessy.

"Would you like to have a go, Dessy?" Andy asked. He handed a club to Dessy.

"Start with just the one," he said, "to get the feel of

it. You hold the handle, like this – then flick it up into the air. OK?"

"Game ball," said Dessy. He flicked the club upwards and it sailed high into the air, turning over and over. Then it came down. Dessy reached for it and missed, and the club landed on his toe. "Yow!" said Dessy, holding his foot and hopping about.

Molly had a go, and managed to catch the club, but only by using both hands.

"Well, you've made a start," said Andy. "Now, I'd better get on with some practice myself."

"Yes, Andy, you need practice, I'd say." The voice came from Paula, who had stopped beside them. "You're not quite as slick as you used to be."

"Perhaps *you'd* like to have a go," said Andy sharply, offering her the clubs. But Paula knew she could never compete.

"All in good time, Andy," she said, and walked on towards her own caravan.

Molly and Dessy decided to follow her at a distance, just in case they could pick up some kind of evidence of what she and Enzio were up to.

Her caravan was parked beside the big horse-box truck, which had PAULA'S PRANCING PONIES painted on the side. At the back of the truck a wire fence had been put up to make a kind of paddock in the field. It was big enough for Paula to practise riding the ponies around. At the moment the two ponies were standing side by side, their heads down as they chewed at the grass.

They saw Paula go into the paddock. She was carrying a leather riding crop like jockeys use. Dessy and Molly knew she would chase them off if she saw them, so they crawled under the truck. Crouching down, they had a good view of the paddock.

Paula went up to one of the ponies. It lifted its head, then it seemed to back away. Paula put a bridle over its head, struggling a bit as the pony resisted.

They heard her say: "Stay still, Lara, you fool!"

"Lara doesn't seem to like her much," said Molly.

"That horse has good taste," said Dessy.

They watched Paula leap on to Lara's back and grasp the reins. Then she gave the pony a tap with her riding-crop, and it began to trot round the paddock. After circling the paddock twice, Lara stopped and began munching the grass.

"Go on, Lara! Go on!" snapped Paula impatiently. The pony took no notice.

"I said GO ON!" Paula shouted. Then she gave the pony a hard slap with the crop, then another. It raised its head and pawed the ground. Paula shouted again, and again slapped the leather crop down hard. Lara began trotting round, now and then raising her head to whinny. Paula slapped the crop down hard each time, and the pony went on trotting – panting and snorting as it did so.

"She shouldn't treat it like that!" Molly was angry. "I'm going to stop her!"

She started to crawl out from under the truck, but Dessy held her back.

"Not now," he said. "It won't do any good. She'll just bar us from the Circus field, and carry on being cruel to the ponies."

"Then we must tell someone."

"Not Enzio, he'd take her side."

"And Andy's got enough problems with Paula – she'd just be meaner to him than ever."

"I know," said Molly. "What about that woman who has the performing dogs?"

"Madame Gazeba."

"Yes. She just loves those dogs, you heard how she was talking baby-talk to them. She'll be really angry when she knows how Paula is treating her ponies."

"OK, let's track her down."

Madame Gazeba was just leading her two dogs down the ramp out of the truck.

"What beautiful dogs, Madame Gazeba," said Molly. "What are their names?"

"You like dogs, do you?" Madame Gazeba was pleased.

"I love them," said Molly. "We have a very clever sheepdog at home, called Tina."

"And what's *your* name?"

"Molly. We have the grocery shop in Ballygandon. And this is my friend Dessy."

"How do you do? Meet Tizzy Wizzy and Toozy Woozums, the best performing dogs in the world! Shake hands, doggies!"

Immediately, the two dogs sat down, and each of them held out a paw. Molly reached down and shook one, and Dessy the other.

"Pleased to meet you," said Molly.

"Howya?" said Dessy.

"There's something we want to tell you," said Molly.

"Tell me on the way to the Big Top," said Madame Gazeba, "We're just going to rehearse. Come along, doggies!" She led the dogs between the trucks and caravans towards the huge striped tent. On the way, Molly and Dessy told her what they had seen.

"No, no, you must have been mistaken," said Madame Gazeba. "Circus people are never cruel to their animals. No creatures are going to perform well if they are frightened. Paula may have tapped them with her riding crop, but she wouldn't hit them hard."

"But we saw her . . ." Molly said.

"You young people imagine things," said Madame Gazeba. "It's to your credit that you care so much about animals. Why don't you come and watch my rehearsal, and you'll see how circus people really treat their little friends."

"We'd love to," said Molly. It was clear again that

they would need real proof if they wanted to convince Madame Gazeba of what they had seen.

They followed her as she led the dogs through a flap in the tent, and into the circus ring. They looked around in wonder. The tent arched high above them, and two trapezes hung from high up in the roof. On each side there was a tall ladder which led up to a tiny platform.

There were ranks of red seats sloping upwards all around the low parapet that enclosed the ring, which was strewn with sawdust. At one side of the ring was a shallow tank on wheels, with glass sides. The two seals were slumped in the water, their heads just out of it. Madame Gazeba went across and patted each of them on the head.

"Hello Lolly, hello Polly," she said. "It will be your turn soon. Say hello to our friends here. Bark, bark!" Obediently, the two seals raised their heads and made a honking sound.

Molly and Dessy laughed, and honked back.

"You two can be my assistants for the rehearsal," said Madame Gazeba. "Go and get that gear from over there and bring it to the middle of the ring, would you?"

She pointed to the side, where there were two round hoops on stands, two pairs of stairs, and a striped football. They dragged the hoops and stairs into the centre of the circus ring, then Dessy dribbled the ball across too. Then they stood to one side to watch.

Madame Gazeba cried: "Hoop-la!"

At once, one of the dogs bounded across to the foot of the stairs, scampered up them and jumped through the hoop. The other dog followed ... Madame Gazeba picked up the second hoop and held it out about six feet from the first. "Hoop-hoop-hoop-la!" she called. This time the first dog jumped through the first hoop, landed on the ground, and immediately leaped high in the air through the second hoop. Again the second dog followed.

Molly and Dessy clapped.

"Take a bow!" said Madame Gazeba. The two dogs stood up on their hind legs and began to walk around the ring, yapping.

"Aren't they brilliant?" Molly laughed.

The dogs walked back to Madame Gazeba, and she gave them a biscuit each, and patted them on the head. "You see," she said, "kindness works wonders. Circus people are never cruel to animals."

Molly knew she was wrong. But how could they prove it? They must find a way. In the meantime, Molly had another plan of her own. A plan to train her dog Tina to be a star of the Circus ring ...

CHAPTER SIX

Beware the Chocolates!

The next morning, Molly and Dessy were out in the yard in front of the grocery shop.

The black sheepdog, Tina, was asleep in the sunshine.

"I've got some dog-biscuits ready to reward her for the tricks," said Molly.

"We'll have to get her to *do* the tricks first," said Dessy, eyeing the sleeping dog doubtfully.

"Tina is very intelligent," said Molly, defending her, "she'll have no problem. First we must get a hoop for her to jump through, and I know just the thing. A bicycle tyre! We'll take one off one of my brothers' bikes."

"They won't be too pleased."

"They won't know. They're staying at my uncle's place for another two weeks. So is my little sister."

*   *   *

51

They went into the shed and levered a tyre from one of the bikes. They brought a wooden box out too.

"Now you sit on that, Dessy, and hold out the tyre." She went across to the dog and knelt down, saying: "Wake up, Tina! Good girl! Wake up!"

The dog raised her head, looked sleepily at Molly, and gave a couple of wags of her tail. Then she put her head down and went back to sleep.

"Oh, she's intelligent all right!" Dessy smiled. "She'd rather sleep than caper about doing silly things."

"I'll show *you*, Dessy!" Molly was annoyed. "Tina will be a star!"

She finally succeeded in waking Tina and persuading her to go across the yard. Dessy sat on the box, holding the hoop a metre above the ground. Molly left Tina and went to the far side of the hoop. She held out a dog-biscuit.

"Come on, Tina! Jump!" she called.

Tina got up and ambled across the yard. She walked straight under the hoop, ignoring it altogether. Then she went over to Molly and took the biscuit.

Dessy was tempted to make a joke, but he wisely said nothing.

"We'll have to put her through the hoop first," said Molly, picking up the dog.

They spent most of the morning showing Tina what she was supposed to do. But apart from consuming a large number of dog-biscuits, Tina didn't seem to get very far with her circus training.

"If only she could talk," said Dessy, "we could do a stand-up routine together." He turned to the dog and said: "Hey, Tina – what did the sheepdog say that made the lamb run away in fright? Now Tina, *you* answer: 'CHOP, CHOP!'"

"You're a hoot, Dessy," said Molly.

They heard Brendan's voice calling: "Hi, there!" They turned towards the gate and greeted Brendan and Locky.

They all went inside and sat around the kitchen table. Tina followed, hoping for a few more dog-biscuits.

Brendan and Locky reported on their conversation with Hans.

"He just won't believe Enzio is planning to take over," said Locky. "If we could only get some proof . . ."

"Maybe this is it!" said Brendan. He reached into his hold-all and produced the box of chocolates. He took off the lid. "A present to Hans – from Enzio! Luckily Hans gave them to us."

"Lucky is right!" said Dessy, reaching for a chocolate.

"Stop, Dessy, you eejit!" said Brendan. "Don't you realize, they might be poisoned! Enzio could have given Hans the food poisoning that put him into hospital, and now he wants to make him worse – maybe finish him off altogether."

"That's a bit dramatic, isn't it?" said Molly. "Even Enzio surely wouldn't go as far as murder?"

"We won't know, until we can get those chocolates tested," said Brendan.

"How do we do that?" Dessy asked.

"We could always use Dessy as a guinea-pig," Molly suggested. She grinned and pushed the open box towards him. Dessy looked tempted.

"Don't even think of it!" said Brendan. "Strange as it may seem, we'd hate to lose you." He took the box away and put it down on the chair beside him. "Now, let me tell you what my father said about checking up on the field with the planning people."

They listened to Brendan, and decided that while they waited to see what his father could discover, they would have to try to find out more about Mrs O'Rourke and Seamus's plans for the field.

Suddenly, Locky said: "Hey, watch out! Look at Tina!" He pointed at the dog, who had her paws up on the chair and was munching at the tray of chocolates.

"Stop her! She'll be poisoned!" cried Molly, rushing round and hugging Tina.

Brendan snatched the box of chocolates away and put them back on the table.

"How many has she eaten?" asked Molly.

"Two or three, it looks like," said Dessy.

"What shall we do?" said Molly. "Maybe we should make her sick." She was sitting on the chair now, with the dog on her lap. Tina was wagging her tail and looking longingly at the chocolate box.

Locky said: "Let's wait a few minutes, and see if she shows any bad signs. If she does, we can rush her off to the vet."

They went on talking about the investigations they wanted to make, but none of them could help glancing at Tina now and then.

After ten minutes, Tina was still sitting happily on Molly's lap, and gazing at the chocolates. Locky said: "Looks like it was a false alarm."

Molly put her face close to Tina's, and said: "Are you all right, Tina? Tell us you're not poisoned!" The dog gave a loud bark, and began wagging her tail and licking Molly's face vigorously.

"It seems the chocolates are OK," said Locky.

"Great!" said Dessy, reaching out and putting one in his mouth.

Brendan, Molly and Dessy decided to visit Andy at the Circus, to tell him about the meeting with Hans.

"I'll bring my camera," said Brendan. "I can take some action shots of Andy juggling."

Locky said he'd stay and have a chat with Molly's mother.

As they went along the road leading to the field, Brendan stopped suddenly. He pointed up towards the castle and said: "I wonder who that is, up on the hill?"

In the distance they could see two people sitting on the hill, just below the castle. They had something spread out in front of them, and one of them was pointing to the circus field down below. The other was looking through a pair of binoculars.

"They're probably just visitors, having a picnic," said Locky.

"They seem vaguely familiar," said Brendan. "I've got a long-focus lens on my camera, I'll take a look at them." He adjusted the camera and focussed it on the hill.

"Well, well!" he said. "It's Seamus and Mrs O'Rourke. I wonder what they're up to."

"Let's find out," said Molly. "We can go round to the far side of the hill and get up to the castle that way. Then we can hide behind the wall. They're quite near to that ruined window."

When they reached the castle, they crouched down behind the window and peered over the ledge. Seamus and Mrs O'Rourke were sitting with their backs to them, side by side, gazing down at the field below. The Big Top towered in the centre, and the caravans and trucks clustered around. It reminded Brendan of western movies, with circles of wagons.

"You don't suppose . . . ?" Molly began in a whisper, then paused.

"Suppose what?" asked Brendan.

"Well, that maybe Mrs O'Rourke and Seamus are a number?"

"They *are* a number," said Dessy. "Two!"

"Shut up, Dessy!" Molly was impatient. "I mean, do you think they've got a romance going?"

"WHAT?" Brendan was stunned.

"Ssssh!" said Molly. "They'll hear us."

"A romance?" Brendan whispered. "What a horrible idea. I mean, they're as old as the hills."

"Ancient," said Dessy. "They're well past it."

"Try and hear what they're saying," said Molly. "It might be lovey-dovey stuff."

They craned their heads over the ledge and listened.

"We should get the OK from the planning people within a week," said Mrs O'Rourke.

"How did you persuade them?" Seamus asked.

"The deeds. I gave them the deeds. They show I own the field."

"Do you think they'll be fooled?" Seamus chuckled.

"Why wouldn't they be? I got prizes at school for copying. I copied the whole lot. All I had to do was change a name or two. They look just like the original deeds."

"Not much lovey-dovey stuff there," said Brendan. "It sounds a lot more sinister."

Seamus bent down and picked up something spread out on the ground in front of them. From below they had thought it might be a picnic table-cloth, but as Seamus held it out in front of him, they could see it was a large map.

"Imagine," he said, "all this will be down there, on that field!"

"What's on the map, can you see?" asked Dessy.

"No, it's too far away," said Molly.

"I know!" said Brendan. "I'll take a long-distance picture!" Quickly he focussed the camera, and leaning on the ledge, pointed it towards the map. He clicked, and clicked again.

"What was that?" said Mrs O'Rourke. She turned in their direction, but they ducked down just in time.

"What was what?" Seamus asked.

"I thought I heard something, up there in the castle."

"You haven't started believing in ghosts all of a sudden?" Seamus laughed.

"Of course not. But I'm going to have a look." She began to walk up the hill towards them. Seamus followed.

"Run for it!" said Brendan, and the three of them ran off, scrambling and stumbling among the stones scattered on the ground.

They got down the hill and made their way into the Circus field. They leaned against the nearest caravan to get their breath back.

"That was close," Dessy panted.

"Could you see what was on the map?" Molly asked.

"Not exactly," said Brendan. "But it looked like diagrams of houses and roads."

"So that's what she's planning for the field," said Molly.

"What's more, it sounds as if she's got no right to do it," said Dessy. "Remember what she said about deeds and copying and changing names?"

"We'll have some proof when I get this film developed," said Brendan. "I'm going to ride into the town. They've got a one-hour place there."

"Right," said Molly. "We'll go and see Andy."

They found Andy in his caravan. He looked depressed. They told him what Brendan and Locky had said about the visit to Hans.

"Hans was always very trusting," said Andy. "That's why his circus people are all so loyal to him. Well, almost all of them . . ."

They told him about their climb up to the castle and what they had seen and heard.

"When Brendan gets back we may have some proof at last," said Molly.

"I wish we could get some proof about Enzio and Paula's plans," said Andy.

"We're working on it," said Dessy.

"It may be too late, unless I can get my act together properly," said Andy.

"What do you mean, Andy?"

"I can't explain it, but when I was rehearsing today, nothing would come right. I did everything the way I always do, but I seemed to be suddenly all clumsy. The clubs just wouldn't go right. Maybe it's all this worry about Hans and the plots against him and me. Or else . . ."

"Yes, Andy?" Molly wondered.

"Well, it sounds crazy, but when I was juggling, it almost seemed as if there was something interfering with the clubs. Some kind of evil magic . . ."

CHAPTER SEVEN

Car Crazy

"Do you mean some evil spirit has got into the clubs?" asked Molly.

"I know it's hard to believe," said Andy, "and of course Circus people are very superstitious. It just felt as if someone else was flinging the clubs around, as well as me."

"We've known some odd things happen around that Castle, all right," said Dessy.

"It's a weird place."

"Do you suppose . . ." Molly looked thoughtful.

"Suppose what?" Andy asked.

"Well, you know that jester Andreas who tried to warn Princess Ethna? He was killed there. If he *does* haunt the castle like they sometimes say, maybe his spirit is jealous of another juggler coming on the scene."

"You're making my hair stand on end," said Dessy.

"It does that already," said Molly, trying to joke, although she was really quite alarmed herself.

"Maybe you could leave out the juggling," said Dessy.

"I can't do that, it's my star turn." said Andy. "But we've got to look on the bright side: at least the other parts of my act are OK."

"What else do you do?" Molly asked.

"Lots of clowning," Andy said. "I've got a load of props. Why don't you lift up that canvas cloth there?

They looked at the cloth, which was covering a large bulky object standing beside the caravan. Molly lifted one edge and Dessy the other, and they pulled the canvas away.

"Wow! That's some car!" said Dessy. They gazed down at the strange vehicle. It looked like a ramshackle old jalopy that someone had dragged from a junk-heap.

It was a two-seater open car with no roof, and the sides and the bonnet were all dented and bashed in. It was painted with splodges of bright colour – red, yellow and blue.

"I'd better try this out, in case some ghostly racing-driver has put a spell on it," said Andy, trying to make light of it all. He stepped over the driver's door and sat down in the seat, the big rusty metal driver's wheel in front of him.

"Do you fancy a trip?" He pushed open the passenger door, which creaked on its hinges. Molly and Dessy squeezed into the seat beside Andy. "Right, away we go!"

Andy started the engine which made a chugging sound. Then he honked a loud horn that was fixed to the side of the car. With a rattle and a backfiring roar, the car began to trundle round in a circle on the patch of ground outside Andy's caravan.

Molly held on to the dashboard and Dessy to the side door as they were bumped about while the car trundled over the rough ground.

Suddenly it came to a halt. There was a loud bang, and a great jet of water gushed into the air out of the front of the bonnet. It was splashing down all over them. Molly and Dessy crouched down, shrieking, as Andy produced a large red umbrella and opened it over them all.

"Just a little hiccup," said Andy. "She'll be right as rain soon!"

"We've got the rain already!" said Dessy, laughing.

"Hold on tight," said Andy. Dessy held on to the side door as Andy pressed a lever. There was another bang, and both the doors fell off. Dessy tumbled out on to the ground. Andy pressed another lever, and the entire seat collapsed backwards. Molly found herself lying flat on her back in the car. She sat up and scrambled out.

She and Dessy laughed with delight as they watched Andy first of all take hold of the driving wheel, which came completely away in his hands. Then there were more bangs, and the wheels collapsed. Then the bonnet flew off and landed with a clatter on the ground. Soon Andy was standing in the ruins of the car. He leaned down and picked up a large bottle that looked like champagne.

Then he stepped out of the car and shook it vigorously, like the winners do at the end of Grand Prix races. There was a pop and a spray of liquid came jetting out of the bottle. Andy waved it around so that it sprayed over Molly, Dessy and himself.

Then he made an extravagant bow.

Molly and Dessy applauded loudly. Then they heard a slow hand-clap beside them. It was Paula.

"Lovely act, Andy," she said. "It went a lot better than your juggling rehearsal just now."

"You saw that, did you?" said Andy sourly.

"I just happened to be passing," said Paula. "Maybe you should stick to the clowning. It suits you better."

"Thanks for your advice," said Andy sarcastically. "Maybe I'll discuss it with Hans when he comes back."

"If he comes back," said Paula. Before Andy could say any more, she strode away.

"Where did you get that fantastic car?" asked Dessy.

"I made it myself. You can help me put it back together, ready for the opening show this evening."

When Molly and Dessy got back home, Locky said: "Come and see what Hans has sent from Dublin." They went into the shop. In the middle of the floor there was a large wicker hamper. The lid was open, and Molly's father was carrying things from the shelves and putting them into the hamper. They peered inside. Around the sides, standing up, were several champagne bottles. Molly's father was stacking the centre part of the hamper with boxes of chocolate, cakes, fruit and sweets.

"The champagne was already in it," Locky explained. "But Hans sent a load of money so that your Dad could fill it with extra things from the shop. It's all going down to the field so the Circus people can celebrate the opening performance."

"I wish the Circus came here more often!" said Molly's father. "That Mr Hopper is very generous."

"He wrote saying he wanted to thank the family for their concern," said Locky.

"Hey, look at those bottles," said Dessy. "Maybe we could use one to try that trick Andy did, and squirt the stuff over everyone."

"Hands off," said Molly's father. "This is all going to the Circus today."

Locky had bought them all tickets for the performance. He said he had recently had a lucky win at the races. "It was a horse called Trapeze Artist," Locky said. "I couldn't resist it."

"We'll be seeing the real trapeze artists later," said Molly excitedly. "The Flying Phantoms."

"As long as they don't fly any real ones in from the haunted castle," said Dessy.

They went back into the house, and soon Brendan arrived back from the town.

He produced the packet of photographs. "Look," he said, "there are some great action shots of Andy juggling."

"He hasn't been juggling so well since then," said Dessy. They told Brendan about Andy's problems with the clubs.

"Does he really think it's the ghost of Andreas messing about?" asked Brendan.

"He doesn't want to believe it," said Molly, "and he admits that circus people are very superstitious. But he can't think of any other explanation."

"Perhaps he really has lost his touch, and he's trying to make excuses," said Dessy.

"Paula and Enzio would be only delighted if that was true," said Molly.

"I wonder if they could be mixed up in it," said Brendan. "We'll have to do some more detective work on that. Meanwhile, we do have some evidence about what Mrs O'Rourke and Seamus are up to."

He showed them the two photographs he had taken of the map Seamus was holding out. They were really close-up, thanks to Brendan's long-distance lens. They could see that the map was definitely a plan for a housing development. It had a network of roads, and plots marked out with diagrams of houses in the middle of each. They could even see the way the inside of each house was divided into rooms.

At the top of the map in big letters were the words CASTLE VIEW. Below this they saw:

Twenty superb luxury homes.
Owner: Mrs J.O'Rourke. Manager: S.Gallagher

"I'll ring your father tonight," Locky told Brendan. "I'll tell him what we overheard about the forged deeds. His planning contact can check the real deeds."

"But the real deeds are probably missing," said Brendan. "Mrs O'Rourke must have copied them and changed the names, then given in her fake ones instead."

"That means she has the real ones hidden somewhere," said Molly. "We'll have to track them down. More work for the Ballygandon Private Eyes."

"Well, whatever tracking we have to do," said Dessy, "I'm not going to miss the Circus!"

"There's no way we'll miss that," said Molly.

"What did the detective say when he solved the robbery from the bakery?" Dessy asked.

"What did he say, Dessy?" Locky asked.

"It was just a piece of cake," said Dessy.

The Circus was due to start at seven o'clock. Mrs

Donovan began fussing at around five-thirty, making sure that everyone was washed, and dressed in clean clothes. She fussed as much about Locky as she did about everyone else, because he insisted on wearing a long yellow ostrich feather stuck in his hat.

"It looks ridiculous!" said Molly's mother.

"*Flamboyant* is the word I'd use," said Locky. "It looks right for the Circus."

"They'll think you're one of the performers."

"All the better, I can step forward and give them my number."

"What number is that, Grandpa?" asked Brendan.

Diddle-diddle-dumpling, my son John
Went to bed with his trousers on.
One shoe off, and one shoe on,
Diddle-diddle-dumpling, my son John!

"That's terrific, Grandpa!" said Molly.

"It's childish," said her mother.

"Then it probably suits my mental age," said Locky cheerily. "But wait till you see the dance."

"Take no notice of him," said Molly's father, "he's just sending you up. Now, is everyone ready? Locky, you can go in the car with us, and the kids can walk."

"We'll take the short-cut across the fields," said Molly. "See you there." She was out of the door before her mother could say anything about not getting her dress muddy.

* * *

68

"I bet they're all tucking into that hamper by now," said Dessy. "I wish they'd let us take it, we might have been able to share it."

As they went along the paths that led through the fields, they could hear the rowdy music coming from the Circus, and the cries of "ROLL UP! ROLL UP!" When they reached the road near the gate, they could see Mrs O'Rourke in her anorak, directing the cars towards the parking area at the far side of the field – and collecting money from the drivers.

"How mean can you get?" said Brendan. "She's already making a fortune from hiring the field."

"Not to mention the fortune she'll make from the houses," said Molly.

"She may not be so lucky there," said Brendan. "Locky told my father we suspected the deeds might be a forgery, and he's going to alert the planning people."

"But unless they can find the real deeds, how can they prove anything?" Dessy wondered.

"That's why we've got to find them," said Brendan.

People chuckled at Locky's feathered hat as he held out the tickets and led his group through the entrance. There was a buzz of excitement from the audience in the ranks of seats all around the ring under the Big Top. The music blared loudly, as they pointed things out to each other: the tall vertical ladders that led up to the dangling trapezes, the hoops and stairs for Madame Gazeba's dogs, the balloons strung in a line, each with a luminous letter on, to read HANS HOPPER'S CIRCUS, the glittering stars hanging from the striped roof way above them.

Suddenly the music stopped and all the lights went out. There was a gasp from the audience. Then there was a drum-roll, and a single spotlight beamed down on the centre of the circus ring. Standing there was a tall figure in a bright red coat, white trousers and knee-length black boots. He was wearing a shiny black top hat, and holding a long whip in his right hand.

They saw the moustache, and recognized Enzio, the Ringmaster. He raised the whip and flicked it down. It gave a deafening crack. Then his voice came roaring through the loudspeakers: "LET THE CIRCUS BEGIN!"

CHAPTER EIGHT

On With The Show!

Enzio cracked his whip again. They all blinked as suddenly the bright lights came on in the Big Top, and the blaring circus music filled the tent. At the same time a spectacular procession entered, and marched around the sawdust ring, waving at the crowd, while Enzio stood in the centre, whirling his whip around his head.

First in the procession came Paula, standing in her carriage in her dazzling costume, and urging on the two ponies. This time they were relieved to see she used only the reins and no riding crop. Next came the trapeze artists, the Flying Phantoms, dressed in black skin-tight costumes with luminous skeletons painted on the front of them.

The whole circus troupe followed. Madame Gazeba led her two performing dogs, walking on their hind-legs, each done up with fancy pink bows tied to their heads.

The Dragon-Man held a blazing torch which he

whirled around his head. The tightrope walker came on, doing cartwheels and then a handstand. A man in a turban carried a big transparent box in front of him.

"What's in there?" asked Locky, pointing.

Brendan and the others peered. "It's got silver and black zig-zag markings," he said. Just then the object in the box moved, raising a pointed head and sticking out a forked tongue.

"It's a snake!" Dessy cried.

"I hope they don't open the box," said Locky. "I'm allergic to snakes."

"He'll have to open it for his act, Grandpa," said Molly. "He's a snake-charmer."

"Well, he doesn't charm *me*," said Locky. "I prefer the giant behind them."

They looked at the amazingly tall figure who came next. It was dressed in a long crimson cloak, and must have been at least five metres tall. The smiling face of a girl with short green hair peeped out from the collar at the top.

Suddenly she undid the collar and the cloak fell away, revealing three people standing on each others' shoulders. They jumped down and began turning somersaults in the ring.

Dessy said: "Hey – what did they call Count Dracula when he flew out of his tomb doing a somersault?"

"What, Dessy?" asked Locky.

"An Acro-BAT!"

The procession continued, until finally the audience laughed excitedly as Andy the Clown came on. He was in his bright spotted costume with baggy trousers, and was wearing the long shoes which flapped at the end. He was balancing a plastic bucket on the end of a long stick. Suddenly he pretended to trip. The bucket wobbled and swayed, until with a flick of the stick Andy made it turn upside down. There was a splash, and a flood of whitewash splattered down all over him.

Andy stood there for a moment, his clown mouth turned down in a mock frown.

Then he ripped off his soaking costume and cast it aside, to show that underneath he was wearing a smart black suit with a floppy green bow-tie. He ran around the edge of the ring, showing the tie to the children in the front row. As they leaned forward to look closer, the tie squirted water at them. There were shrieks and laughter as Andy circled the ring, then went flap-flapping out in his long shoes.

"Well, that's a relief," said Molly, "Andy's act has gone all right so far."

"Let's hope his juggling does too," said Brendan. "That comes right near the end."

They watched with delight as the various circus acts performed in turn. The Flying Phantoms hurled themselves into the air, the Dragon-Man breathed fire, the snake-charmer played a recorder and his snake rose up from the box and writhed about in time to the music.

Paula's ponies pranced on their hind-legs, Madame Gazeba's dogs jumped through their hoops, and the seals played a game of netball, flapping about and balancing the ball on their noses. The acrobats leaped and somersaulted about, and the tightrope walker danced along his rope high up in the Big Top.

One of the biggest hits was Andy's collapsing car. Once again they were relieved that the act had gone according to plan.

Then towards the end of the show, Andy appeared in his juggling clown costume. It was covered in spangles that flashed in the lights, and had a white ruff at the neck. He was wearing red trainers instead of his long flapping shoes, and he had a battered red bowler hat on his head, with a tall feather sticking out of it.

"He's copied my hat!" said Locky.

Andy put the tatty hold-all he was carrying down on the ground, and took out his clubs one by one, holding each of them up in the air as he did so.

There was a drum-roll, and the lights went down, so that there was just the one spotlight on Andy. He began to fling the clubs into the air and catch them, keeping up the complicated pattern, as though the clubs were dancing in the air.

"He's doing all right," said Molly.

Then suddenly one club seemed to slip in his hand, and fell to the ground. He reached to catch the next, but it fell at an awkward angle and he missed it. Then he leaped up for the third club, and the fourth, but they both seemed to slip out of his hand and fell to the ground.

The audience laughed. They thought this clumsiness was just a part of the clowning. Andy realised what he must do. He fell flat on his face among the clubs. Then he began clowning about with them, picking one up and trying to balance it on his finger, then standing on one leg and putting a club standing on his toe, over-balancing backwards and falling to the ground.

As he went on clowning, Brendan suddenly said: "Look, over there at the entrance."

Just inside the gap in the tent where the performers came in, they could see Enzio and Paula. They were peering in at the show. Then they saw them turn to each other and begin making angry gestures.

"What's up with them?" asked Dessy.

Just then, they saw Paula turn and stomp away into the darkness behind. Enzio strode into the ring. He cracked his whip and called out: "Thank you, Andy!"

Andy glared at him, finished his act and stuffed the clubs back in his hold-all. Then he raised his hat and waddled off, while the audience clapped.

The show finished with another big parade. Brendan, Molly and Dessy told Molly's father and mother they would like to go backstage and see their friend Andy. This took a bit of persuading, but they finally agreed.

Outside, the four of them went round the tent,

threading their way carefully among the stretched wires and ropes that held up the Big Top. They went past the rows of caravans till they came to Andy's. They knocked on the door.

"Yes, who is it?" asked Andy gruffly.

"It's just us – the Ballygandon Gang," said Molly.

Andy opened the door. He was halfway through taking off his clown make-up, and his face was smeared with a smudge of colour and face-cream. He began wiping it off with a towel, and said: "Come in, come in!"

"You were great, Andy," said Molly, as they sat down round the table. "The car was fantastic," said Dessy.

"Sure, sure. Thanks," said Andy gloomily. "And then there was the grand finale. How to drop your juggling clubs in one easy lesson!"

"You were brilliant," said Locky. "I don't know what happened with the clubs, but you made the best of it. Everyone just thought it was part of the show."

"Enzio knew it wasn't," said Andy. "That's why he came on and wrapped up the act. I could tell he was angry that I'd managed to cover up."

"Maybe that's what he was arguing with Paula about," said Molly. They told Andy about what they had seen.

"They want me to mess up, that's for sure," said Andy. "But how could they have anything to do with it? I really felt tonight as if some outside power was monkeying about with the clubs. And just in case it *is* that Andreas up in the castle, I'm going up there tomorrow to confront him!"

They looked at Andy, startled. He really seemed to believe that the spirit of Andreas had it in for him. But supposing he was right . . . ?

There was a loud rapping at the door. They heard Enzio's voice outside.

"Andy! I want a word with you!"

Andy told them quietly, "Stay here. I'll handle it." He went out of the door, and they heard him say: "Yes, Enzio, what seems to be the problem?"

The four of them bent their heads down over the table so that Enzio wouldn't see them through the window.

"You know very well what the problem is," said Enzio. "Your juggling has gone to pot. You've simply lost it, Andy."

"The audience didn't seem to think so."

"You covered up well, I'll give you that. But we both know you couldn't handle those clubs at all. And if you weren't one of Hans's favourites, I'd give you the sack right now. I'll have to tell him about it of course."

"Do you really need to . . . ?"

"Of course I do. He's the boss after all – for the moment."

"What do you mean, for the moment?" Andy asked angrily.

"Never mind," said Enzio. "But just remember – if you mess things up again, you're out!"

They arranged to come and see Andy the next day, and go up with him to the Castle. He still seemed to be convinced that there was some kind of presence lurking there, which was messing up his act. He was going to challenge it.

The four of them walked along the row of caravans. When they were a hundred metres away, they saw a strange figure sneaking along behind the caravans. It wore a raincoat and a peaked cap pulled down, and looked furtively around as it moved along.

"Let's stop and wait," said Brendan.

The figure reached Andy's caravan, went up the steps and tried the door. It wouldn't open.

Whoever it was didn't go away, but reached into the pocket of the raincoat for a key. Before putting it in the lock, the figure looked around again and caught sight of their group. They could see the face clearly. It was Paula. Seeing them, she quickly put the key back in her pocket and hurried away.

"What was she up to?" wondered Dessy as they approached the caravan.

"Up to no good, that's for sure," said Brendan. They knocked on the door but there was no reply. Then they saw Andy coming towards them.

"I got a message to go and see Enzio," he told them, "but he wasn't there."

Inside the caravan, they told Andy what they had seen. "It looked as if she had a key and was going to let herself in here," said Molly.

"I've got the only key, as far as I know," said Andy. "Besides, what would she find in here? There's nothing much to steal."

"Perhaps she's the one who's been messing up your clubs," Molly suggested.

"We'll soon see," said Andy, opening the hold-all and taking the clubs out. He examined them closely, and tossed them about from hand to hand. "They seem perfect to me," he said, "and yet when I was out there in the ring, I couldn't control them. But maybe we'll soon find the true explanation."

"Where?" asked Locky.

"Up at the castle. Come on!"

Just as they were getting up to go, Andy's mobile phone rang. He picked it up, and smiled.

"Hans! Hello, how are you?" As he listened to the reply, he began to look depressed.

"Yes, I suppose Enzio had to tell you. Hans, I can't explain it. The clubs just wouldn't work properly for me. Yet they seem fine now . . . Yes, I'm sure it won't happen again . . . I'm going to sort it all out, believe me . . . Yes, I'm sure of it. When will you be back?"

He went on talking to Hans for a short while, then hung up.

"Hans still doesn't know when he'll be let out of the hospital," he said. "He told me he had every confidence in Enzio to keep things going."

"I wish I could say the same," said Locky.

"So do I," said Andy. "But there's no point in sitting around whingeing. Let's get up to the Castle."

Even in daylight, the inside of the Castle felt cold and spooky. They gazed up at the ruined tower where Princess Ethna had been murdered.

"Imagine," said Molly, "Ethna came here to be married. She expected that her children would grow up and play here in Ballygandon, just as I did. Her new husband Prince Fergal was a kid here." She went across to the ruined window and looked down the hill at the field and the tents and caravans. "Perhaps they had fairs and festivals down in the field all that time ago, and he and the other kids went and played there."

"Perhaps Andreas the Jester went and joined them," said Brendan.

"Andreas, yes indeed!" said Andy. "I'm going to put him to the test." He took the set of clubs out of his bag. "This is where he stood, isn't it, juggling, trying to warn the Princess up in the tower?"

"That's right," said Molly, "just below the tower. That's what the legends say."

Andy went and stood in the exact spot. The tower

80

rose up behind him, as the others watched him begin to toss the clubs.

"OK, Andreas," cried Andy, "Do your worst!"

CHAPTER NINE

Haunted Clubs

They watched Andy toss the clubs one by one into the air, until all four of them were tumbling and turning at the same time, with Andy catching them expertly and flinging them up again.

"Isn't he great?" said Brendan.

"It almost beats yo-yo tricks," said Dessy.

Suddenly they noticed a puzzled look come over Andy's face. He kept juggling away with the clubs, but first one, then the others, started to soar much higher than before. Andy dodged around, looking way up into the air to make sure he could catch each one and launch it upwards again. Higher and higher the clubs went, higher even than the top of the tower.

Now Andy was smiling with eager excitement, as he kept his eye on the clubs and went on catching and throwing, catching and throwing. As they sailed upwards and downwards, the clubs even seemed to make extra little twirls and somersaults in the air. Andy was breathing quickly with the exertion of it all. Once he let out a triumphant cry of: "Fantastic! Fantastic!"

Brendan took some photographs. He had to kneel down right at Andy's feet to get a shot of the clubs whirling high up near the top of the tower.

After ten minutes of the most spectacular juggling, Andy kept hold of each club as it came down, till he was holding two in each hand. "Wow!" he said.

"Andy, that really *was* fantastic!" said Molly.

"Out of this world," said Brendan.

"Game ball," said Dessy.

"Well, if Andreas's spirit was there, trying to mess you about, you certainly beat him," Molly said.

Andy said seriously: "Oh, I have a feeling that he was there all right, but urging me on, not messing me about – and giving me a helping hand!"

"Do you really think so?" Brendan was startled.

"What else could explain it? I've never done juggling like that before. The clubs were going so high I thought they were going to come down with ice on them!"

"I wonder if Andreas could juggle like that with his silver clubs," wondered Molly.

"Wouldn't it be great if we could find them?" said Dessy. "They must have fallen around here somewhere, if this is where he was juggling before they came to kill him. Why don't we try digging for them?"

"I don't think there'd be much point," said Brendan.

"Whoever killed Andreas wouldn't pass up the chance of pinching the clubs. All that silver on the handles would be worth a lot."

"Yes, I should think it was prized off and melted down long since," said Molly.

"Well, they obviously couldn't melt *him* down!" said Andy. Then he raised the clubs in the air with both hands, looked up at the tower and said: "Thanks, friend!"

When they reached the bottom of the hill, Andy told them he would go and stow his clubs in his caravan, then he was going to the Dragon-Man's caravan to have a drink with him and Madame Gazeba.

"Could you do me a favour?" Molly asked.

"Sure," said Andy.

"Well, I was wondering if you could ask Madame Gazeba if she'd help me train Tina to do some tricks."

"Certainly I'll ask her. I'm sure she'll give you what tips she can."

"Wonderful!" said Molly. "I can go and get Tina now, and introduce her."

"I'll tell Madame Gazeba to expect you – in say, an hour or so," said Andy.

When he had gone off to his caravan, Brendan said: "Well, you've got a nerve, Molly!"

"You don't get anything unless you ask," said Molly brightly.

85

"But do you really think Tina can be trained?" said Dessy. "Remember what happened when we tried her with the hoop. She had about as much cop-on as a dead elephant."

"You're an eejit!" snapped Molly. "Stick to your stupid yo-yo tricks!

"I'll go and get Tina on my own!"

She ran off up the road.

"I'll go after her," said Dessy.

"Bad idea," said Brendan. "You really upset her, Dessy, you clown. You know how she dotes on that dog."

"Yeah," said Dessy. "I'll tell her I'm sorry. But between you and me, Brendan, Tina has as much chance of learning a trick as flying to the moon. She's very affectionate and all that, but as thick as two short planks."

"Well, don't say that when you apologise, that's my advice."

"Fair enough," said Dessy. "Hey, what did the puppy that was brought up with a bunch of kittens, say when it wanted to be fed?"

"I don't know, Dessy."

"BOW-MIAOW!"

Brendan was silent.

"Well, you're a great audience, I must say," said Dessy.

"Sorry, Dessy, I wasn't listening. I just saw someone, over there on the other side of the road, behind the hedge."

"Who?"

"I'm not sure. It looked like Mrs O'Rourke."

"Well, isn't that one of her horse-drawn caravans in that field?"

"Yes, it's an old disused one that's falling to bits. Let's take a look through the hedge."

They went across the road that led between the Circus field and the field behind Mrs O'Rourke's house. They peered through the hedge. They could see Mrs O'Rourke, just climbing up the steps into the ramshackle old caravan. It was nothing like the smart motorised caravans the Circus people lived in. It was an old-style, barrel-shaped caravan with big wooden wheels, that used to be drawn by a horse when she hired it out to holiday-makers.

"What's she going in there for?" Dessy wondered.

"Let's find out," said Brendan. They crept through a gap in the hedge, and across to the caravan. Then they hid underneath, between the wheels. They could hear voices inside the caravan above them.

"I rang up today," Mrs O'Rourke was saying. "The planning permission should be through to us tomorrow."

"So they don't suspect anything about the deeds?" said a man's voice.

Brendan and Dessy glanced at each other. They recognized the growling tones of Seamus Gallagher.

"Not at all," said Mrs O'Rourke. "I told you I did an

expert job. I wasn't worried about that. All I was afraid of was that they might say it was some kind of historic site, like the Castle, and put a preserving order on it."

"Why should they? It's only an old field, after all."

"And a very profitable field it's going to be, eh, Seamus!"

Seamus laughed. "You can say that again."

As they listened, Dessy was sitting with his back against one of the wheels. Suddenly he felt one of the spokes give way. There was a crack and the spoke came away from the wheel. The caravan lurched slightly.

"Get out, quickly!" Brendan cried. "It's going to fall down and crush us."

They scrambled out from beneath the caravan. It didn't come crashing down, but it had certainly tilted.

Seamus and Mrs O'Rourke were equally alarmed. They came rushing out of the caravan and stumbled down the steps.

"Hey, you! What are you doing?" shouted Mrs O'Rourke, as she spotted Brendan and Dessy as they started to run.

"Come here!" yelled Seamus. With surprising speed, he rushed across the field and launched himself at Brendan. With a floundering attempt at a rugby tackle, he fell flat on the ground. But he had just managed to clutch on to Dessy's ankle. He held on to it hard, as Dessy struggled. Mrs O'Rourke came over, and they pinned Dessy down.

Brendan looked back, and stopped running.

"OK," said Dessy. "You've got me!" They let him get up, as Brendan came back.

"What were you doing, spying on us?" Seamus asked menacingly.

Brendan decided to brazen it out. "We know what you're up to. We've seen the plans."

"Where? How?" Seamus was furious. He turned to Mrs O'Rourke and said:

"You told me only you and I and the planning people had seen them!"

"Keep your temper, Seamus!" said Mrs O'Rourke. "I don't know how they saw them."

"We spies have our methods," said Dessy in a sinister tone.

"They're probably bluffing," said Mrs O'Rourke, "but anyway, it doesn't matter now. The plans will be public as soon as we get the OK tomorrow. Then there's nothing anyone can do about it."

"What about the park and the playground?" said Brendan angrily. "Wouldn't that be better for Bally-gandon?"

"Who cares about Ballygandon?" snarled Seamus. "This will be much better for *us*!"

"Even with forged deeds?" said Brendan coolly.

Mrs O'Rourke went white.

Seamus roared: "Forged deeds! What do you mean,

you sneaky little horror?" He raised his fist, ready to smash it at Brendan.

"Stop!" said Mrs O'Rourke. She looked icily at Brendan and Dessy, then smiled a thin smile. "Now we know you are bluffing. You just try telling that to the authorities. They'll realize you're just making it all up to rubbish us. Do you think they're going to believe a couple of snotty-nosed kids? Go on, get out of here!"

Brendan and Dessy ran back across the field and through the gap in the hedge. They peered back through the gap. They could see Mrs O'Rourke and Seamus talking earnestly to each other. They looked very worried.

"I think we put the wind up them," said Brendan proudly.

"They're running scared," said Dessy.

"The problem is, they're right – we haven't got any proof, and those planning people aren't going to believe a bunch of kids. If only we could find the original deeds . . ."

"Look, there's Molly," said Dessy, uneasily. "I'd better go over and say I'm sorry."

They went along the road to meet Molly, who was just approaching the gate to the Circus field. She had Tina with her on a lead. She went straight past them without speaking, and began to open the gate.

"Listen, Molly, I'm sorry," said Dessy, "I didn't mean what I said about Tina. She's a grand intelligent dog, aren't you, Tina?" He bent down and stroked the dog's head. Tina barked enthusiastically.

Molly was nearly won over, but she decided not to make peace just yet. "All right, Dessy. Then say sorry to Tina."

"What?"

"Tell Tina you're sorry."

"OK." Dessy knelt down beside the dog and put his mouth to her ear, saying: "Tina, I'm sorry. You're the brightest dog in the world. I'm going to put you on my team at the next Table Quiz."

Tina turned to Dessy and licked his nose. "There!" said Dessy, patting the dog's head. "I think she's forgiven me."

"She's a very generous dog," said Molly. "Now before we go to see Madame Gazeba, I want to try and rehearse Tina in a few tricks. Let's go over to the far corner of the field there."

As they went, Brendan and Dessy told Molly about their meeting with Seamus and Mrs O'Rourke.

"We've got to stop them somehow," said Molly.

When they reached the corner of the field, Molly produced a bag with some dog-biscuits in it. "She used to be able to sit up and beg," she said. "That would be something at least to show Madame Gazeba. Come on, Tina, there's a good girl . . ."

Molly held out a biscuit. "Beg for it, Tina!" she said.

The dog barked and wagged her tail. Then she jumped

up and tried to grab the biscuit. Molly let go of it, and it fell to the ground. Tina began to paw the ground as she looked for the biscuit in the grass. Then she started to dig with her paws.

"She thinks it's got buried," said Brendan, trying to cover up a smile.

Tina eagerly went on digging a hole in the ground. Molly called: "Tina! Tina!" but the dog took no notice. Dessy and Brendan looked on, silently.

They couldn't think of anything to say that would not put Molly in a temper.

Tina continued to dig, scattering the earth about behind her. Then she gave a yelp, and stopped. She looked down into the hole, whimpering a little, and held up a paw.

"There!" said Dessy. "She's begging!"

"Nonsense!" said Molly. "I think her paw is hurt. There, there, Tina, it's all right . . ." She held Tina's paw and examined it. "It doesn't seem to be bleeding or anything, she must have hit it on a stone."

Brendan knelt down and looked into the hole. "It looks more like a piece of metal," he said. He took out his pen-knife and scooped away at the earth around the object. Then he took hold of it and eased it out. He held up what looked like a small statuette, caked in mud. He scraped some of the mud away.

"It's quite heavy," he said, "and it looks to me as if it's meant to be a model of some kind."

"It looks like a horse," said Dessy. "See the four legs there."

"I wonder what it's made of," said Brendan. He scrape carefully with his pen-knife. Something gleamed. "Wow, it could be silver!" he said.

"I know!" Molly exclaimed. "Remember what I was saying about the family in the Castle, and wondering where the kids played. Perhaps it was here. Perhaps this is one of Prince Fergal's toys!"

Molly took the small horse from Brendan and gazed at it.

"Could be," said Dessy. "Only a Prince would have a toy horse made of silver."

"It must be very old," said Brendan. "Hundreds of years old."

"And if it is," said Molly triumphantly, "there may be lots more things buried here, like when they found the Ballygandon Hoard up in the Castle. And that means it's a historic site. They'll never let Mrs O'Rourke build her houses here now!"

"We'll have to get somebody to look at this, and check that it really is old," said Brendan.

"And I know just who we should get," said Molly. "Come on – we've no time to lose!"

CHAPTER TEN

The Priceless Toy

"Who do you mean?" Brendan asked Molly.

"Gemma Danaher. That friend of Locky's who's a historical expert."

"The one who came to look at the ancient monument in the grounds of the home where Locky lives?"

"That's right – and she got kidnapped and locked up in it!"

"She did," said Dessy, "so maybe she won't be too eager to help *us* again!"

"I'm sure she will," said Molly. "Come on, we must find Locky and ask him to call her."

Molly took off her anorak and wrapped the horse statuette in it carefully, while Brendan took pictures of the site so they would know where to find the spot again.

*   *   *

They had just come out of the field and were hurrying up the road when a van passed them. It stopped twenty or thirty metres ahead.

"That's Mrs O'Rourke's van, isn't it?" said Molly. She was right. Mrs O'Rourke got out and began to stride towards them. There was no time to get away. Soon she was standing in front of them, her hands on her hips and an angry scowl on her face.

"I was just going up to your shop," she said to Molly. "I want to tell your parents to keep these hooligans in order!"

"They've done nothing wrong," said Molly. She held the bundled anorak behind her. She didn't want Mrs O'Rourke discovering what they had found – at least, not yet. But Molly had reckoned without Tina. As they argued, the dog began sniffing at the anorak. Then she started barking excitedly.

"You should keep that wretched dog under control!" said Mrs O'Rourke. "It's a menace."

"Quiet, Tina, quiet. Good girl . . ." said Molly. She turned and patted Tina's head, trying to hold the bundle away from her. But the dog snatched at it, and pulled the anorak away, so that the statuette fell on to the ground. Tina snuffled around it, delighted. Molly picked it up.

"What's that?" asked Mrs O'Rourke.

Molly had to think quickly. If she told the woman where they had found it, she would claim it belonged to her. So she said, "One of the Circus people gave it to us as a souvenir. It's just an old ornament." Before Mrs O'Rourke could examine it, Molly wrapped it up again in the anorak.

"If that mob gave it to you, it's probably stolen," said Mrs O'Rourke.

"They're not to be trusted."

Molly thought: "You trust them enough to screw a lot of money out of them" – but she said nothing.

Mrs O'Rourke said: "When I tell them about your lies and your bad behaviour, I hope your parents will teach the three of you a lesson!" Then she turned and went back to her van.

"How are we going to contact Locky?" said Brendan. "We'd better not go back home just yet."

"We can phone him from the telephone box in the main street," said Molly.

But when she tried to reach Locky at Horseshoe House, she was told he was on his way to Ballygandon.

"We're in luck. Look up the road." Brendan pointed.

Locky's car was making its rattling way towards them. They waved, and he stopped beside them. "Can we take a drive around, Grandpa?" said Molly. "We've got something to tell you."

"Sure. Jump in."

*   *   *

As Locky drove through the countryside, they told him about their find. Locky stopped the car. He examined the statuette, and said: "I'll ring Gemma right now."

He fished his mobile phone out of his pocket.

After the conversation he said: "She was very interested. She said she could come down tomorrow."

"I must get those photographs of the site developed," said Brendan.

"OK, I'll drive you into the town now," said Locky. "We can have some tea while we wait."

The batch of photographs also included the pictures of Andy juggling. "Those are spectacular shots," said Locky. "I'm sure they'll convince Hans that Andy hasn't lost his touch."

"Let's send him copies today," said Brendan.

"Even better, I'll take them to him," said Locky. "I was going to go up to see him soon anyway. I'll go on the evening train. I have a little plan for when he comes out, to make sure he really knows what's going on in the Circus."

"I hope he'll be coming out soon," said Brendan. "otherwise Andy could be in dire trouble."

Brendan was right. In spite of Andy's wonderful juggling performance at the Castle, when it came to the Circus show that evening, the clubs once again just wouldn't behave properly.

The three of them went round to see him afterwards.

"I just can't understand it," Andy said. "I don't know what's going wrong."

"At least we know it can't be anything to do with Andreas," said Brendan.

"Perhaps I *am* losing my touch." Andy looked really depressed.

"We don't believe that," said Molly.

"That Paula woman has something to do with it, I reckon," said Brendan. "We must keep our eyes on her."

"Our *Private* Eyes!" said Dessy.

Just then they heard a loud rapping at the door, and Enzio's voice outside called:

"Andy! We need to talk. I'm coming in."

"It might be best if he doesn't see you," said Andy. "Quick, duck in among those costumes on the rack."

They went over to the costume rack and stood huddled behind the row of clown outfits. The door opened and Enzio came in. He glared at Andy and said: "Well, what have you got to say for yourself?"

"I can't explain it, Enzio. The clubs just wouldn't go right tonight. Yet this morning when I was practising, everything was brilliant."

"So you say," said Enzio sarcastically. "but of course that wasn't in front of an audience, so I've only your word for it."

Brendan wanted to step forward and say there *had* been an audience, the Ballygandon Gang, and Andy *was* brilliant. But he just had to keep his mouth shut.

Enzio continued going on at Andy, getting more and more insulting. Finally Andy couldn't take any more.

"You've no right to slag me off like that!" he shouted. "OK, I've had a couple of bad nights, but you know the rest of my act is great, and the audience loves it."

"Yes, the *rest* of your act!" Enzio snarled, "and the rest of your act is all you're going to be doing for the rest of this visit."

"What do you mean?"

"I mean for the rest of our shows here you'll just do the clowning. Paula will do a juggling act instead."

"Paula?" Andy couldn't believe it. "She can't juggle her way out of a paper bag."

"Don't you say a word about Paula, or you'll be out altogether – now!" said Enzio. "Tomorrow she takes over the juggling, and that's that!"

"Wait till Hans hears about this," said Andy.

"Oh, he'll hear about it all right," said Enzio. "I'm going to call him in the morning. And he'll also hear that after we finish at Ballygandon, he's going to have to hire a new clown!"

Enzio went out, slamming the door of the caravan.

As they stepped out from their hiding place among the costumes, Brendan trod on something. He bent down, and picked up a chunky ear-ring.

They went across and sat at the table with Andy. "I

found this on the floor," said Brendan, putting down the ear-ring. "Maybe it's part of your costume."

"No, it's not mine," said Andy. "But it looks familiar."

"Perhaps it's Madame Gazeba's," said Molly.

"No," said Andy thoughtfully. "I think it belongs to Paula."

"We'll have to keep a watch on Paula," said Molly as they waited the next day for Gemma Danaher to arrive. "She's obviously been getting into Andy's caravan and doing something to mess up his clubs."

"But then how come Andy could juggle so well when he was at the Castle?" asked Dessy.

They looked at one another. "I guess he had some help," said Brendan.

Gemma Danaher was delighted to see them all again. At the kitchen table she examined the statuette excitedly, carefully brushing away the earth that was clinging to it. She held it up and turned it one way and another, admiring it.

"Well, this is really quite a find!" she exclaimed. "It looks like a silver horse, maybe for a child to play with – and at a guess I'd say it's hundreds of years old, from about the time of the original Ballygandon Hoard."

"It must be very valuable then," said Dessy.

"Oh yes, priceless!" said Gemma. "Can you show me

where you found it? There might be more treasures buried there."

She drove them towards the Circus field, but Molly said: "It might be better to leave the car a little way away, in case Mrs O'Rourke notices it and wonders what we're doing going into the field." She told Gemma what they knew about Mrs O'Rourke's plans, and what they had heard about the forged deeds.

"Well, this treasure you've found should put a stop to her housing development," Gemma said, "at least until we've made a detailed study of the land, and found what else might be buried there."

Gemma Danaher parked the car, and put the statuette in the glove compartment. She locked up the car and they walked to the gate of the field. Checking with Brendan's photographs, they led Gemma to the exact spot where they had found the treasure.

Gemma knelt down and with a small trowel she began to scrape away at the earth around the hole that Tina had dug. Molly had thought it better not to bring Tina on this particular excursion. The dog was an enthusiastic digger, but not exactly a careful one.

"We'll need to get a proper team down to probe the site," Gemma said. "Meanwhile, I'd better ask the owner to rope off this area, to preserve it."

"She won't be too pleased," said Brendan.

"We won't know till we ask her," said Gemma.

"Well, now's your chance!" Dessy said.

Mrs O'Rourke was striding towards them across the field.

"What are you lot doing in my field?" she shouted. Then seeing Gemma she said: "And who are *you*?"

Gemma explained. Mrs O'Rourke looked more and more annoyed as Gemma told her that the finding of the treasure could delay any development of the site.

"It's all nonsense!" she said. "These kids are lying to you. They told me they got that horse thing from one of the circus people."

"I don't think so," said Gemma. "I think they found it here, in your field."

"Let's have another look at it then."

"We haven't got it with us at the moment," said Gemma. "But I'm convinced it's genuine. I'm going to take it to Dublin tonight to get it examined. Then we will have to make a proper survey of the site."

"Will you now?" said Mrs O'Rourke. "Well, just try it on, that's all! I'll have you booted off the field in no time!"

She turned and marched off to the gate. They saw her get into her van and drive away. Gemma asked Brendan to take some more photographs of the site and the surroundings.

They walked up the road and got into Gemma's car. Molly sat in the front seat.

As Gemma started the car, Molly opened the glove compartment to look at the statuette. The compartment was empty.

CHAPTER ELEVEN

Caravan Secrets

"The horse has gone!" Molly exclaimed.

Gemma stopped the car. "It can't have. Let me look, it must be behind those maps and tapes." She leaned over and rummaged in the glove compartment, swooping out the contents. Then she said: "It must have fallen on the floor. We'll get out of the car and hunt for it."

They all got out. They peered and groped on the floor underneath the seats, and looked in the side pockets and under the dashboard. There was no sign of the statuette.

Dessy said: "Hey, look at the catch on this back door. It's all scratched. I reckon someone forced it."

"It must have been done by the robber who took the horse," said Brendan.

"And I guess we all know who that must be," said Molly.

"Yes," said Gemma. "Mrs O'Rourke. She's the only

one who'd want to get rid of the statuette, because it would hold up her plans. Where does she live?"

"In that house at the far end of the field," said Molly.

"I'll go and see her. If she won't give the statuette back, I'll tell her I'll call in the Guards." She got into the car, saying: "It's probably better if I go on my own. If I have to tell the Guards it may take a bit of time."

"We'll go down to the Circus and see Andy," said Brendan.

"I'll see you at the Circus field gate in an hour," said Gemma. She drove away.

"I'll go and get Tina," said Molly. "I never got to show her to Madame Gazeba yesterday. I'll bring her down now."

"We'll warn Madame Gazeba," said Dessy.

"What do you mean, *warn* her?" Molly frowned.

Dessy said hastily: "Oh, I mean let her know. I'm sure she'll be very pleased."

Molly suspected Dessy was being sarcastic, but she decided to let it go. "See you down there, then!" she said, running off up the road.

Brendan and Dessy found Madame Gazeba sitting outside her caravan with the Dragon-Man. There were two cups of tea on a folding table in front of them.

Madame Gazeba said she would be happy to see Molly's dog, but the Circus business was hard enough to get into for humans, and even more difficult for animals.

"What tricks can your friend's dog do?" she asked.

"Well . . ." said Brendan desperately.

"She can bark very nicely," said Dessy.

"There was a troupe called the Singing Dogs once," said the Dragon-Man. "They could bark that song, *How Much is that Doggie in the Window*."

"They were a hopeless bunch," said Madame Gazeba loftily. "My doggies are much more refined."

She poured some more tea, and said: "I'm afraid it's rather lukewarm by now."

"I'll soon fix that!" said the Dragon-Man dramatically. He took a swig from a flask beside him, lit a match, and breathed a jet of fire at the cup. "There!" he said, as the others looked on in astonishment.

"Look over there," said Brendan suddenly. "Locky's back." They saw Locky walking between the caravans. Walking beside him was a man in a long coat and a black felt hat. He had a bushy ginger beard and moustache, and carried a walking stick.

"I wonder who that is," said Dessy.

"We must tell Grandpa about the statuette," said Brendan. He was about to go across, when Locky saw them and waved. The two men came over to them.

"This is a friend of mine from Horseshoe House," said Locky. "Harry Skipper."

He introduced them all.

Brendan told him about Gemma and the theft of the statuette.

"I hope it turns up, so that we can delay their plans," said Locky, "especially after what your father told me in Dublin. His contact in the planning department said they could do nothing unless the real deeds turn up. As far as they were concerned, the ones they have are all they've got to go on."

"Didn't Dad tell him they were forgeries?"

"Yes, but he said that was only a claim, nothing could be proved."

"We've got to find those deeds, and the statuette," said Brendan.

"Well, Harry and I are going to take a stroll around the Circus," said Locky.

"We're coming to the show this evening. I see Paula over there, exercising her ponies. Come on Harry, let's go and watch."

"I hear Paula is going to do the juggling act instead of Andy," said the Dragon-Man. "If you ask me, there's a bit of a fling going on between her and Enzio."

"Really?" Harry Skipper seemed interested.

"Oh sure," said the Dragon-Man, "how else would she get to do the act?"

"How interesting," said Harry Skipper. He and Locky moved on.

Soon afterwards, Molly appeared with Tina.

"So this is your performing artist?" said Madame Gazeba. "How do you do?" She held out her hand.

"Go on, Tina," said Molly. "Shake hands."

Tina barked and began licking the outstretched hand. "She usually does it all right," said Molly. Brendan and Dessy looked at each other and raised their eyes.

"How high can she jump?" asked Madame Gazeba.

"Oh, quite high," said Molly, "but she might need a bit of help."

"I see what you mean," said Madame Gazeba. She looked at Tina, who was now lying on the ground, her eyes closed.

"Do you think you could train her?" asked Molly.

"Well," said Madame Gazeba, "it would certainly be a challenge. I tell you what, you go home and see what tricks you can teach her, and we'll have another look at her in a few days' time."

"Thank you," said Molly, disappointed. "Come along Tina, we'll go and see Andy."

They found Andy outside his caravan, talking to Locky and Harry Skipper.

"I couldn't believe it," said Harry, "she was vicious to those ponies."

"We told Madame Gazeba," said Molly, "but she said circus people were never cruel to animals."

Locky said: "Madame Gazeba is an old softie. She really pampers those dogs of hers."

"Perhaps that's the answer," said Molly eagerly.

"What is?" Dessy asked.

"To getting dogs to do tricks. Madame Gazeba talks to her dogs like babies. I'll try it with Tina." She knelt down and tickled Tina's ear, cooing: "There, there, Tina-Wina, does oo like to have oo's ear tickled then? There's a sweety-tweety doggie-woggie!"

"Pass me the sick-bag," Dessy muttered.

"I've got to practise," said Andy. "I must make sure I can still handle those clubs."

They watched him perform his juggling act. He tossed the clubs expertly, and they twirled and tumbled just as he wanted.

"That's very impressive," said Harry Skipper. "I can't understand why Enzio wants to replace you."

The Ballygandon Gang explained their suspicions about Paula messing about with the clubs.

"But why are they all right now, and not when you do the show?" asked Harry.

"I don't know. She fixes them somehow, I'm sure. We found her ear-ring in my caravan."

"We'll need more proof than that," said Locky.

"I think I know how we could get it," said Brendan. He held up his camera. "I'll hide in the caravan and take a picture. But that will only work if Andy is doing the juggling. Otherwise she'll have no need to mess with the clubs."

"We'll see how she makes out tonight," said Andy. "I

reckon she'll be barred after one performance. At least, she would be, if only Hans were here."

Brendan wondered why Locky was smiling.

They met Gemma at the gate. She was furious. "That woman has really got a nerve!" she said. "She denied everything. She even laughed when I told her I was going to make a statement to the Guards."

"What did the Guards say?" asked Brendan.

"They were sympathetic, but they said they couldn't do anything without proof. It was only Mrs O'Rourke's word against ours. I've told the department people in Dublin about the statuette, but they can't do anything about making the field a historical site, if there's nothing historical to show for it."

She said she would go into the Circus field to say hello to Locky, but then she had to get back to Dublin.

As they began walking back towards Molly's house, the Ballygandon Gang were gloomy.

"I suppose we could break into Mrs O'Rourke's house," said Brendan. "She must have the statuette hidden somewhere."

"Unless she's thrown it in the river," said Dessy.

"You're a right cheerer-up, you are," said Molly.

"OK, here's a joke to cheer you up then," said Dessy. "A man went into a Chinese restaurant. 'Do you do take-aways?' he asked the fellow running it. And what do you think he said?"

"Don't know, Dessy," said Brendan.

"He said: 'Certainly sir. Take away five from twenty, and you've got fifteen!'"

"If I knew the Chinese for HA-HA . . . I wouldn't say it!" said Brendan.

"Tina, stop! Come back!" cried Molly, as Tina rushed off and darted through the gap in the hedge opposite. She pushed her way through the gap and began running after the dog. Brendan and Dessy followed.

Tina was running about in the field, sniffing the various smells delightedly. As they got near to her, Molly called: "Come here, Tina!" The dog looked up and barked happily, then ran off again. She was making for the broken-down caravan.

Before they could reach her, she had run up the steps and inside. They clambered up carefully after her, one at a time, in case the rickety steps gave way. The inside of the caravan was dark, the only light coming through cracks in the roof where bits were missing. It was very dusty, with a rusty sink and a cooker covered in grime, and at the far end a table with cushioned benches around it.

Tina was barking and sniffing, and she managed to slip away each time Molly tried to grab her. Then she snatched one of the cushions off a bench, and started to drag it about the floor. It seemed to be quite heavy.

She bit and tore at it excitedly, as if she had found a bone inside. As the fabric was torn away, they saw something gleaming.

"Give it here, Tina, good girl!" Molly cried, kneeling down and grabbing the cushion. But the dog wouldn't let go. She thought it was a new game. There was a tug-of-war. Suddenly there was a ripping sound, and the cover of the cushion was torn in half. With a thud, the statuette dropped on to the floor.

"We've found it!" Brendan shouted, holding up the figure.

"Tina found it!" said Molly. "Now who says she isn't an intelligent dog?"

Molly petted Tina, who was still chewing at the inside of the cushion. She pulled something out and began chewing at it. It was a sheaf of papers.

"Tina, give me that!" said Molly, snatching the papers. She gazed at them.

"There's a map with them," she said. "It says CASTLE FIELD. It looks like the same area as the one on the picture of the map you took, Brendan."

"I know what those must be," said Brendan. "The original deeds!"

Just then they heard a voice outside the caravan. "Mrs O'Rourke? Are you in there?" It was Seamus Gallagher.

CHAPTER TWELVE

Mystery Man

They looked round wildly. The open door was the only way out, and they could see the burly figure of Seamus coming up the steps. Molly stuffed the statuette back into the cushion cover and held on to it. Brendan put the sheaf of papers down the front of his shirt.

"Are you there?" said Seamus, peering into the dark of the caravan. "I've come about my share of that money . . ."

Then he saw them. "What are you lot doing in here?"

"Nothing, Mr Gallagher," said Molly calmly. "Just exploring."

Seamus Gallagher looked down and saw the torn pieces of cushion on the floor. "You found them!" he snarled angrily.

"Found what, Mr Gallagher?" Brendan smiled innocently.

"The deeds of course!" Brendan wondered whether

Mrs O'Rourke had told him about the statuette. Probably not. She might well be planning to sell it off later, without saying where it came from.

"What deeds?" asked Dessy. "Do you mean daring deeds, or glorious deeds, or dirty deeds . . . ? We haven't done any of those."

"Stop acting the maggot!" Seamus growled. "I know you've got them. Give them here!" He lunged first at Molly, grabbed her arm and began to twist it behind her.

At once there was the sound of fierce barking, and Tina sprang at Seamus Gallagher. He gave a cry of pain as the dog grabbed his leg in her jaws. He let Molly go and tried to beat Tina away, but she held on.

"Get her off, get her off me!" he shouted.

"OK, Gang, run for it!" cried Molly. They all dashed past Tina and down the steps of the caravan. Molly stopped at the bottom of the steps. "Here, Tina!" she called. The dog let go of Seamus's leg and ran out of the caravan. She was barking excitedly. She stood up on her hind legs and licked Molly's face.

"Good girl, Tina, good girl!" said Molly, patting her head. Seamus limped to the door of the caravan.

"I'll get you, I'll get you!" he shouted. But as he began to come down the steps, Tina turned from Molly and started barking and snarling at him. He retreated into the doorway of the caravan. "Get that mangy dog away from me!" he said.

"You stay right where you are, Tina," said Molly, holding Tina's collar and kneeling at the bottom of the steps. She turned to Brendan and Dessy, saying: "I'll keep Seamus here while you go and find Gemma Danaher. Give her the horse to take back to Dublin, and the deeds too. She can pass them on to the right people."

"Right!" said Brendan, and he and Dessy set off across the field. As they scrambled through the hedge, they saw Gemma Danaher near the Circus gate, getting into her car. She was delighted to have the statuette back. She looked quickly through the sheaf of papers.

"Yes, these seem to be the original deeds all right. And as far as I can see, they say the field is part of the Castle land."

"That means it can't be built on," said Brendan.

"Indeed it can't," said Gemma, "and in any case it certainly doesn't belong to Mrs O'Rourke. She could face serious fraud charges over this."

"The field could still be a park for Ballygandon, couldn't it?" asked Brendan.

"Once it's been surveyed to see if there are any more buried treasures, I should think that would be a perfect use for it."

Gemma said she would call the department in Dublin and tell them about the statuette and the deeds, then drive back with them.

"I'm sorry I can't stay to see the Circus," she said. "Locky seems to be having a ball. And at least he can't

117

lose any money betting on circus ponies and performing dogs."

Brendan and Dessy went back across the field to the caravan to tell Molly what had happened. Seamus was still standing in the doorway, looking miserable. Now and then he began to make a move to go down the steps, but each time Tina leaned forward and bared her teeth in a snarl. Seamus was cursing and swearing at the Ballygandon Gang, and especially at Tina, but there was nothing he could do.

"We'll keep him here like this until Gemma is well on the way to Dublin," said Molly.

They waited for half an hour. Then they saw Mrs O'Rourke striding across the field from the direction of her house. "What's going on?" she called out as she approached. "Keep away from that caravan!" Then she saw Seamus and said: "What on earth are you doing?"

"I came looking for you, to get that money you owe me . . ."

"I don't owe you any money!" Mrs O'Rourke cut in.

"We'll sort that out later," said Seamus, "meanwhile, these thieving kids have found the deeds!"

Mrs O'Rourke was furious. "They've found WHAT?!" she yelled. Then she turned to Molly, Brendan and Dessy. "Give those back at once! They're not your property!"

"Nor yours, I believe," said Molly. "In any case, we haven't got them."

"We've handed them in," said Brendan.

Mrs O'Rourke was going red in the face. "You gave them to that woman who came round and threatened me," she cried, "making out she'd call in the Guards!"

"That's just what she did," said Dessy, "and now the evidence has turned up, I reckon they may be asking you to 'assist them with their inquiries'."

"In other words, having you locked up," said Brendan cheerfully.

"We've got to get out of here right away," said Mrs O'Rourke to Seamus.

"How can I, I've got this devil dog trying to savage me!"

"Well, suit yourself!" said Mrs O'Rourke coolly. "I'm leaving anyway." She began to hurry away across the field.

"Wait, wait!" wailed Seamus.

Molly said: "OK, Tina, we'll take pity on him, shall we?" She pulled Tina away a few metres. Seamus staggered down the steps and began to limp off after Mrs O'Rourke.

"Bye-bye, Seamus!" called Dessy. "Have a nice day!"

"They'll never catch up with Gemma now," said Brendan.

"I doubt if they'll even try," said Molly, "they'll be too busy running away from the Guards."

They watched Seamus trying to catch up with Mrs O'Rourke, calling out to her to wait. Then the three of them went to give the news to Locky.

That evening Locky and Harry Skipper were in the audience with them to watch the Circus. Towards the end, where Andy's juggling act usually was, Enzio the ring-master announced: "And now, introducing for the first time a juggling act supreme! You've watched her prancing ponies, you've seen her ride in her carriage, now watch the fantastic skills of JUGGLING PAULA!"

There was a fanfare, and Paula came on, riding one of her ponies. She leaped off its back, and stood in the middle of the ring, with just the one spotlight on her. She juggled with three coloured balls instead of the four clubs Andy used. Then she twirled a plate on top of a long stick, and finally balanced a pile of cups on her head.

The pile began to wobble precariously while Paula tried desperately to keep them balanced. In the end the cups toppled and fell all around her. She curtsied with a flourish, pretending it had been deliberate.

Enzio looked annoyed, but he gave a great shout of: "Now give a big hand, ladies and gentlemen, to the one and only JUGGLING PAULA!" There was some unenthusiastic clapping from the audience, and Paula got back on her pony and rode off.

"She's clueless," said Brendan.

"Dead boring," said Molly.

"Clumsy as a one-legged centipede," said Dessy.

They looked across at Locky and Harry Skipper. Locky said: "I guess you believe me now."

Harry Skipper nodded. His face was grim. He and Locky talked together in low tones, then said they were going backstage to see Enzio in his caravan.

"You can follow on," Locky said, "but keep at a bit of distance. I've an idea we'll need you later, as part of a plan I've got."

As they followed thirty metres or so behind Locky and Harry Skipper, Brendan said: "What did Locky mean about believing him now?"

"Something to do with Enzio and Paula I suppose," said Molly.

"But what's that got to do with Locky's friend, and why are they going to see Enzio?" Dessy wondered.

"We'll soon find out," said Brendan. They saw Locky and Harry Skipper stop outside Enzio's caravan, listening. The three of them took a winding route among the caravans, till they were round at the back of Enzio's caravan, under the curtained window. The window was slightly open, and they could hear the raised voices of Enzio and Paula inside.

"I keep telling you, it was an accident," Paula was saying.

"We can't afford accidents!" snapped Enzio. "You'll

121

ruin the whole plan. Before tomorrow's show you're going to have to practise, practise, practise!"

"Don't you tell me what to do!" Paula was angry.

They heard a knock at the door. "What is it?" barked Enzio, opening it.

Then to their surprise they heard Locky say: "Enzio, Signor Haroldo Skipro, the famous circus impresario, is anxious to meet you. He has plans to invest in you and your company."

"Oh! Really?" Enzio was taken aback. "Come in, come in."

They listened amazed as Harry Skipper in a heavy Italian accent explained that he had been very impressed with the show, and would like to contact the owner Hans Hopper. Then they heard Enzio say that Hans Hopper was sick, and might not be coming back to the Circus. Meanwhile he, Enzio, was totally in charge and able to come to any financial deals Signor Skipro might have in mind.

"What are they up to?" whispered Dessy. Brendan shook his head, puzzled.

"We would like to come back tomorrow and see the show again," said Harry Skipper. "And I believe your clown is a juggler too?"

"Yes, yes, in a way . . ." Enzio said, "but he's not doing it in the show just now."

"Even so, I would like you to include his act tomorrow," said Harry Skipper. Enzio had to agree.

"Good," said Harry Skipper, "well then – buona sera!"

"Good evening," said Locky.

Brendan, Molly and Dessy moved around the side of the caravan. They could see Locky and Harry Skipper walking away. They had their arms round each other's shoulders, and they seemed to be roaring with laughter. Locky looked back, and saw them. He put his finger to his lips, then beckoned that they were to follow.

They followed them past the rows of caravans and through the Circus gate.

Locky got into his car, and Harry Skipper sat in the passenger seat. They leaned over and opened the back door.

When the Ballygandon Gang were in the back seat, Locky began to tell them about their visit to Enzio. Brendan said they had been outside, listening.

Locky said: "Then you'll know that Harry Skipper is really Signor Haroldo Skipro."

"Who in turn is really somebody else entirely!" said the bearded figure.

Locky said: "Meet that master of disguise, Hans Hopper!"

To the astonishment of the three in the back seat, the figure took off the black hat, and with a swift movement, peeled off the bushy beard and moustache.

They saw the smiling face of Hans. "Abracadabra!" he said.

CHAPTER THIRTEEN

Big Top Triumphs

Next morning, Brendan, Molly and Dessy went to Andy's caravan. This time Brendan brought his polaroid camera. They would have an instant picture of Paula when she crept in and began to mess up Andy's clubs. The clubs were in their usual hold-all, which Andy put on the table where the light was bright.

"Now Brendan," said Andy, "if you hide in among the costumes on the rack, you'll be able to poke the camera out to take the pictures when she starts monkeying about with the clubs."

"Then Hans can take the proof to Enzio and Paula," said Molly, "and reveal who Signor Skipro really is."

Andy went out with Molly and Dessy, who crawled under the canvas which covered Andy's collapsible car. Through a gap in the canvas they could see the row of caravans. Then Andy went across to Paula's caravan, to

125

tell her that he was going into Ballygandon, and would be back in an hour in case Enzio needed him.

They hoped Paula would take advantage of his absence to do her fixing of the clubs. They were right. Peering out from their hiding-place, Molly and Dessy soon saw Paula look out of her door to make sure Andy was walking away to the gate.

Soon afterwards she came out of her caravan, wearing the old bulky raincoat they had seen her wearing before. She moved swiftly across to Andy's caravan and went in.

Inside, Brendan watched from among the clown costumes, his camera ready. He saw Paula take Andy's clubs from the hold-all and lay them on the table. Then Brendan got a surprise. Instead of starting to do something to the clubs, she opened her raincoat and Brendan could see that there were big pockets on the inside. From these, Paula began to take out other clubs that looked exactly like Andy's, and put them into the hold-all.

So this was her trick, he realized. She wasn't messing with Andy's clubs, she was switching them for some doctored clubs of her own. After the show when Andy's act had gone wrong, she would sneak in and switch the clubs back again. So, when Andy examined the clubs or practised with them, he would find nothing wrong.

Brendan took a picture. The click of the camera was masked by the clatter of the clubs as Paula put them into the hold-all. Then she started to pick up the real clubs and stow them in the inside pockets of her raincoat. Brendan took another picture.

But this time Paula heard something, and looked up. She listened, staring towards the costume rack. Then she shrugged, and went on stowing the clubs.

Brendan looked at the first picture which was nearly fully developed. He was pleased. It showed Paula clearly, putting clubs into the hold-all. She was caught redhanded! Seeing Paula button up her raincoat and look around the caravan, he shrank further back behind the costumes. Unfortunately, he trod on one of Andy's long clown shoes, and his foot slipped. The noise wasn't loud, but it was enough to alert Paula.

She came across to the costume rack and began groping among the clothes. Her hand touched Brendan's face and she shrieked: "Who's that? Come out of there!"

She grabbed Brendan's collar. Quickly he hid the camera and pictures in the deep pocket of one of the clown suits. Paula dragged him out.

"Oh, it's you – one of those stupid kids who are always hanging about. Well, whatever you think you saw, I'll deny it! And who's going to believe a snivelling little boy? A boy who's just about to get a thick ear!" She raised her hand to hit Brendan. He ducked and she lost her balance. Brendan seized a costume and threw it over her head. She staggered around, trying to free herself.

Unfortunately it was the costume with the camera and pictures in the pocket, and as Paula flailed around, the camera fell out. Paula picked it up.

"A real sneaky detective you are, aren't you?" She said angrily. She looked at the camera. "A polaroid, isn't it? OK, hand over the pictures!" She picked up one of the long clown shoes and came menacingly towards Brendan. He backed away. His foot hit something, and he looked down. It was a plastic bucket full of whitewash, ready for Andy to use in his act.

As Paula was about to hit him with the shoe, Brendan quickly picked up the bucket and tipped the whitewash over Paula's head. She dropped the shoe and screamed, then began cursing as she stumbled around trying to wipe the liquid off.

Hearing all the noise inside, Molly and Dessy decided to act. They clambered out from under the canvas and pulled open the door of the caravan.

"What's up, Brendan? Do you need any help?" Molly asked, looking in. She was astonished to see the figure of Paula, white and sticky from head to toe.

Seeing she was outnumbered, Paula shouted: "Get out of my way!" She pushed past Molly and Dessy and down the steps. They saw her running towards the paddock where her ponies were.

Brendan picked up the camera and groped in the pocket of the clown suit, taking out the two pictures.

"We've got the evidence anyway," he said, "but she's got Andy's clubs. We must get after her!"

The three of them ran after Paula, but she had already reached the paddock. She climbed on to the back of one of the ponies, and giving it a hard slap she rode it out of the gate and through the circus ground. As they followed, they could glimpse the amazed looks of the circus people as they saw this white, flapping figure like some kind of clumsy ghost, go galloping past.

The Ballygandon Gang gave chase, and saw Paula reach the fence at the edge of the field. They heard her cry: "Jump!" as she gave the pony another hard slap. The pony leaped over the fence, nearly tipping Paula off. But she clung on, and rode off down the lane that ran beside the fence.

"That's the way down to the river," said Molly. They reached the fence and climbed over it, then ran down the lane after the pony. When they reached the river they looked along the tow-path that ran along the riverbank. A hundred metres away, Paula had stopped the pony. She was reaching inside her raincoat. One by one she pulled out Andy's clubs and threw them high in the air. They landed with a splash in the river.

"Stop!" called Molly, as they ran along the river bank. But it was too late.

"Well, that will put a stop to Andy's career for a bit," Paula cried triumphantly, as she took off the clammy

129

raincoat and threw it on the ground. "He'll never find those clubs now."

"You won't get away with it," said Brendan. "We've got the pictures."

"I know," said Paula, "and that's just what I'd like you to hand over – or you'll regret it! UP, BELLA, ON YOUR TOES!" She slapped the horse and pulled at its mane. The horse stood up on its hind legs and whinnied. "GO GET THEM, BELLA!" cried Paula, as the horse walked towards them. They looked up at the hooves pawing the air above them.

"Now hand over the pictures or you'll have a hoof on your head!" said Paula.

But before they could reply, something unexpected happened. The horse put its front hooves down on the ground, tossing its head impatiently. Then it trotted over to the edge of the river.

"Back, Bella, back!" cried Paula, but the horse ignored her. It stopped on the bank, with its back to the river. Then it reared up suddenly, flinging Paula off. With a shriek she flew backwards through the air, and landed with a splash in the water.

The pony reared up on its hind legs with a whinnying noise that sounded very like a laugh.

The Ballygandon Gang certainly laughed. "Bella's Revenge!" said Dessy. They watched Paula spluttering and cursing as she made her way over to the river-bank.

"Let's get out of here!" said Molly. She leaped on to

Bella's back and patted her neck. "We'll take the pictures back to Hans. Giddy-up, Bella!" The horse trotted happily along with Molly on its back, while Brendan and Dessy ran along beside them.

They found Locky and Hans waiting in Locky's car outside the main gate into the circus field. Hans was still in his Signor Skipro disguise. They were surprised to see Molly riding the pony. Hans was impressed with how well she handled Bella.

As they stood beside the car, they explained what had happened. Then they showed Hans and Locky the photographs.

"Well, that's firm evidence all right!" said Hans. "Now let's go and see Enzio."

Brendan and the others wondered why Hans was still dressed in his disguise, but they soon found out the reason. They stood outside the caravan listening when Locky and Hans went inside. Brendan dragged a box over and all three of them stood on it. They could just see into the caravan through a gap in the curtains on the window.

"Well, do come in, Signor, you are very welcome," said Enzio in an oily way. "Now about your investment plans . . ."

"We'll come to that later," said Hans, "in the mean time, my friend here has something to show you."

"We thought you'd be interested in these photographs taken in Andy's caravan," said Locky. "They explain why Andy's clubs never seemed to work in the performance. Someone has been switching them secretly for dud clubs."

There was a silence. Then they heard Enzio say: "Paula! That's terrible! I would never have believed it of her."

"You knew nothing about it, then?" said Hans.

"Of course not. I shall certainly give her a stern telling off, and I'll see it won't happen again."

"I think you may have to do more than that, if we are agree terms for my financial deal with you," said Hans. "I have the papers with me, handing over the first instalment to you personally. But I think more drastic action needs to be taken about Paula."

"You mean I should sack her?"

"Exactly."

Again there was a silence. Dessy whispered: "What do you bet he sells her down the river? So much for romance!"

And indeed, when Enzio broke the silence, he said: "Well, if those are the terms you insist on, Signor, so be it. I'll be sorry to lose Paula, but that's show business. Now let's have a look at this deal. As I said, I can take care of the money personally. Sadly, Hans isn't able to do it."

"Is that so?" Hans spoke sharply, and they saw him take off his hat and rip off his beard.

Enzio paled and seemed to stagger. "It's you!" he cried.

"Yes, it's me, Enzio," said Hans. "I couldn't believe you would betray me like this. Without my mate Locky here, and his gang of young friends, you'd have pulled the wool over my eyes. You're leaving the Circus today, and you can take your friend Paula with you."

"I can explain," Enzio pleaded. "It was all Paula's doing. It was her idea."

As Enzio went on trying to wriggle out of it, Molly said suddenly: "Hide, quickly!"

She pointed. In the distance they could see approaching the wet, shambling figure of Paula. They ducked round the side of the caravan out of sight.

Paula came up to the door of the caravan, as they heard Enzio say: "It was all her plan, Hans. I didn't want to go along with it, but she persuaded me."

Paula had heard him too. She wrenched open the door and stormed in. "Oh I did, did I?" she shouted. "You evil two-timer!"

They heard the sounds of a scuffle, then Hans said: "Pack your bags, the pair of you, and be out of here before the show this evening. And leave your ponies, Paula. You're not fit to look after animals at all."

Locky and Hans came out of the caravan, leaving Enzio and Paula scrapping and shouting inside.

"Thank you, thank you all," said Hans. "I'm very

133

grateful. I might have lost the Circus altogether if it hadn't been for you."

"What will you do about a Ringmaster tonight?" asked Brendan.

"I'll be back there in charge of the show myself."

"And what about the Prancing Ponies?" Molly asked.

"Well, I know a young rider who'd be well able to stand in the carriage and drive them, as a temporary stand-in," Hans said, looking at Molly. "That is, if you'll take on the job?"

"Hooray for Prancing Molly!" said Dessy.

"What about Andy's clubs?" said Brendan. "We'll never find them in the river."

"He can probably get a new set by tomorrow," said Hans. "Meanwhile we'll just have to leave out the club part of his act. But what a show we'll have, even so! And tonight, to celebrate my return, I'm going to give free tickets to all the children who'd like to come."

Later they helped Andy clear up the mess in his caravan, while they told him all about what had happened. He said he would get some more clubs sent down from Dublin the next day. Meanwhile he examined Paula's fake clubs with interest.

"She was a better faker than she was a juggler," he said, turning the clubs in his hands. "These look exactly like my clubs, but she has put weights inside them so they fall and tumble in odd ways – and she's put some kind of slippery grease on the handles too. Then after the show as soon as I was out, she must have put the real clubs back again in the hold-all, so I wouldn't suspect anything when I practised."

"She really did want your job," said Brendan.

"Well, she won't get it now, or any other circus work," said Andy. "News gets around quickly in our business. Circus people depend on each other. Enzio and Paula did the dirty on Hans and on me. No one will trust them now."

"I must go and practise with the ponies," said Molly proudly. "I hope I'll be OK in the show."

"You'll be great," said Andy.

"I want to go and take some pictures of the Circus from up on the Castle hill," said Brendan.

"I'll come with you," said Dessy.

"So will I," said Andy, smiling. "I can say hello to Andreas."

Inside the Castle, they stood looking up at the ruined tower, thinking about Andreas and Princess Ethna and all the violent events that had happened there so long ago. Andy went and stood under the tower, throwing imaginary clubs into the air. The wind sighed among the broken stones of the Castle – and as well as the wind, they seemed to hear a faint voice mingled with it, saying in long-drawn-out tones:

"High . . . . High . . . . High . . . ."

They looked at one another. It seemed impossible,

135

but could the spirit of Andreas be trying to tell them something? Andy looked up at the top of the tower.

"High!" he said. "That's it! That's where we've got to look!"

"What do you mean?" Brendan asked.

"High – in the tower," said Andy. "It's just struck me. If Andreas was standing just below the tower here, juggling and trying to give a signal to Princess Ethna, maybe he threw the clubs so they actually landed on the top of the tower, instead of falling to the ground."

"And nobody found them?" said Dessy.

"Could be," said Andy. "It's worth looking, anyway."

They went to the entrance at the bottom of the tower. A stone staircase with a lot of half-broken steps covered in moss, wound in a spiral up into the tower. It looked very dangerous, but Andy began to lead the way up it. They took one step at a time, and kept their backs against the clammy stone wall of the round tower.

Sometimes a loose stone was dislodged, and went crashing down below them. But they finally came to the turret, half of which had fallen away so that the steps led into empty air and the rocky ground many metres below. What was left of the floor of the turret was covered in a mound of leaves and branches and bits of stone.

Carefully Andy leaned forward and began to work at the pile. Piece by piece he took things away. Behind him, Brendan and Dessy looked on.

"There!" cried Brendan suddenly. "I thought I saw something glinting."

Andy scrabbled away faster, and there it was: a juggler's club, with a gleam of silver showing through the grime that coated it. Andy picked it up and turned it around in his hands. "The silver clubs of Andreas!" he said in awe.

He rubbed some of the dirt from the club, and it gleamed even brighter. Gradually he uncovered another club, and then a third and a fourth. He held them up, two in each hand. "Thank you, friend!" he cried.

There was a crash. Part of the turret fell away and landed with a thud below.

"Take care," said Andy. "We must creep down. Take it slowly now. Very, very slowly . . ." Bits of stone came away as they made their way fearfully down the stairs.

Once there was a fierce gust of wind, and Brendan seemed to feel the tower sway. Perhaps the whole structure would collapse, bringing them all down with it.

But finally they reached the bottom safely. Triumphantly, Andy began to juggle with the silver clubs, and now they went up higher even than the last time they'd been at the tower, and twirled and tumbled in the air in amazing ways. Andy laughed delightedly, and they seemed to hear an echoing laugh bouncing around the castle walls.

*   *   *

137

The show that night was a fantastic success. Hans the Ringmaster twirled and cracked his whip, and Molly in a bright green spangled costume rode confidently in, standing in the carriage with the reins of the Prancing Ponies in her hands.

The Flying Phantoms, the Dragon-Man, Madame Gazeba and all the other acts got huge applause from the packed audience. Brendan's parents had come down specially from Dublin. Brendan's father told them that he had been able to write a big story for the paper about the discovery of the treasure and the deeds of the Castle Field. The Guards had captured Mrs O'Rourke and Seamus as they drove towards the airport, planning to try and get out of the country.

Now the other papers and the television cameras had turned up at the Circus Field to cover the story, and discovered the extra bonus of the discovery of even more treasure – the silver clubs of Andreas. The cameras flashed as Andy stepped into the ring and began to juggle with the silver clubs. There was wave after wave of cheering as the whirling clubs sailed high into the Big Top and tumbled down again into the sure hands of Andy.

When he finished his act and took a bow, everyone rose to their feet, clapping and cheering. After a few minutes Hans called for silence. He thanked the audience and said how pleased he was to be back with the Circus and fit and well once more. He thanked all the performers, and said how well Andy had juggled with the silver clubs of Andreas that had been used again for the first time in hundreds of years.

Then he said: "I want to give a special thank you to my friend Locky, and three young people without whom my Circus might not have survived at all. Ladies and gentlemen, let's give a big, big cheer for THE BALLY-GANDON GANG!"

He beckoned, and the three of them came and joined him in the middle of the circus ring, while the cameras flashed and the audience roared. They waved and bowed to the crowd as they stood in the spotlights.

"This is the life!" said Dessy. "Do you think I should tell them my joke about the . . ."

"Just smile, Dessy!" said Molly. "Just smile!"

Published by Poolbeg